FRIENDS
OF ACPL

W9-BRL-366

While the Crowd Cheers

E·P·DUTTON & CO. INC
1852   1953
CREATIVE · 101 YEARS · PUBLISHING

WHILE THE CROWD
CHEERS

All-American Sports Stories for
All-American Boys

BY DAVID C. COOKE

JC7740w

1953   E. P. DUTTON & CO., INC.   New York

Copyright, 1953, by David C. Cooke
All rights reserved. Printed in the U.S.A.

FIRST EDITION

No part of this book may be reproduced in any form without permission in writing from the publisher, except by a reviewer who wishes to quote brief passages in connection with a review written for inclusion in magazine or newspaper or radio broadcast.

Individual Copyrights

While the Crowd Cheers, copyright, 1950, by Columbia Publications, Inc.; *The Star-Dust Kid,* copyright, 1949, by Columbia Publications, Inc.; *Song of the Speedway*—originally titled "Calamity Corner," copyright, 1948, by Skyline Publications, Inc.; *The Big Diamond Feud*—originally titled "The Has-Been Hurler," copyright, 1949, by Columbia Publications, Inc.; *Miracle on the Maple*—originally titled "The Has-Been Hoopster," copyright, 1950, by Columbia Publications, Inc.; *Lightning Rider,* copyright, 1949, by Fictioneers, Inc.; *A Pitch in Time,* copyright, 1950, by Columbia Publications, Inc.

Library of Congress Catalog Card Number: 53-8252

CO. SCHOOLS
C329764

For

JIMMY AND JOEL—

A PAIR OF REAL SPORTS

Contents

Contents

While the Crowd Cheers

While the Crowd Cheers

THE BUS pulled away from the curb with a roar that echoed in the quiet street, and Ted Ryan lowered his heavy suitcases to the sidewalk. He turned awe-struck eyes on the long green campus dotted with shade trees, and the solid, vine-covered buildings beyond. This was Midvale College, the Midwestern seat of learning whose scholarship offer he had accepted over all the rest. The college was small and did not have the heritage boasted by many Eastern universities, but it was Ted Ryan, Sr.'s, alma mater, and that was enough for his eighteen-year-old son who had grown too fast for his years.

Tall, lean, and with an upturned nose in the middle of his freckled face, Ted had been offered the scholarship to Midvale because of his athletic prowess. But his academic marks had also been looked into very carefully, because though Midvale needed the money it could make on athletics, it still wanted its standard of learning to remain at a high level.

Ted was bursting with pride and excitement as he went slowly up the sidewalk, following the faded signs pointing the way to the registrar's office. Then he was in the building, a somber place with composition floors and long, high corridors which made the clacking of his leather heels boom sharply.

He waited on the bench in the registrar's office until

it was his turn, and then sat in the straight-backed chair at the side of a plain desk behind which was seated an attractive girl about a year younger than himself. She had gleaming black hair and smiling eyes, and the sign on the desk said that she was Miss Barbara Cromwell.

Ted introduced himself and took a letter from his pocket. It was from Archibald Monks, prexy of Midvale, and it said that Ted was to be registered tuition-free.

"I received notice that you were coming," the girl said, smiling pleasantly. "Welcome to Midvale. I hope you'll like our little college."

"Oh, I'm sure I will," Ted said. "My father went here too, and he's told me about what a great place it is. I like it already."

They both grinned, and the girl said, "My dad feels the same way. He missed the old college so much that he came back again to be the chemistry professor. It's something that gets in the blood, I guess."

"There are plenty of attractions in its favor, I must say," Ted replied, looking at the girl closely. "Yes, I'm positive that I'll like it here."

Barbara Cromwell leaned over her desk, suddenly very busy. But the smile was still on her face, and Ted thought that he had done very well for his first few minutes at Midvale.

That afternoon, after getting settled in the dormitory, Ted went around to the field and reported to Norman Macrae, the athletic director and football coach.

A little shorter but ten pounds heavier than Ted, Macrae was red-haired and solid. He had been an All-American halfback, and at twenty-five he was one of the youngest college coaches in the country.

"You were due here two days ago, Ryan," he said after Ted told him who he was. "What held you up? One thing I expect you to learn from the start is that I will not tolerate tardiness."

"Sorry, Coach," said Ted, taken aback by the unexpected lashing. "I was working during the summer and had to give notice that I was leaving."

"That's no excuse," Macrae snapped. "We're giving you free tuition, free books, free lodging, and free meals. You're a paid athlete, and you take orders. Understand?"

Ted said, "Yes, sir" numbly.

"Then hurry it up and climb into your uniform," Macrae directed. "I want to see whether you've been a good investment or not." He pointed with a hooked thumb as he walked away. "Take the locker next to Stratton."

Bill Stratton was a blond giant with fair skin and bulging muscles. He grinned and said, "Don't let the coach get under your skin, Ryan. He's a perfectionist and expects everybody else to be one too."

Ted tried to return the grin. "Thanks for the tip. I'm not used to being bawled out that way, and it sort of knocked me back on my heels."

He was knocked back on his heels again when he reached the playing field. The blue-and-white-clad

boys were out there scrimmaging with the second-
string, and when Ted trotted up Norman Macrae
looked him over coldly.

"You don't have much beef for a fullback, Ryan,"
he observed.

Ted said, "I weigh one seventy. That seemed to be
enough in high school."

"But this isn't kid stuff any longer," Macrae said. "In
case you haven't heard, this is college football and the
competition is tougher."

Ted's Irish anger suddenly boiled, and he said tartly,
"Then what do you want me to do—just wait around
till I put on more weight?"

Macrae's head jerked up and his black button-eyes
flashed. "You'll do what I say, Ryan. Now get in there
for Adams and show me what you've got."

Until meeting Norman Macrae, Ted had felt excited
about his scholarship to Midvale, but now the excitement was gone and there was only resentment. He
understood that he was nothing more than a piece of
meat to be put on the scales and weighed, with the
prospect of being discarded if he was found wanting.

"Never mind specific plays," Macrae told the players. "Just give Ryan the ball and let him run."

They huddled and Ted said to Ernie Prentiss, the
diminutive quarterback, "Nice guy, this coach."

"Like a rattlesnake," Prentiss whispered. "He's ready
to strike all the time. What do you want to try,
Ryan?"

Ted said an off-tackle plunge, and the huddle broke.
Hank Smith got down over the ball and Ernie Prentiss

rattled off the signals. Then the ball was in Ted's hands and Macrae's acid remarks were forgotten.

The hole was opened by Blimp Friedman and Larry Hall, the big right guard and tackle, and Ted was into it in a flash. Joe Bailey, the maroon-jerseyed second-string quarterback, tried to stop him, but Ted straight-armed him as he snake-hipped through. Les McBride and Bert Sharp, the speedy ends, cut down two of the backfield men, and the field was clear with the exception of the fullback.

Macrae blew his whistle and halted the play. "All right," he said when Ted came back, "so you were lucky. The second-string line was weak. But it won't be like that when we meet King, I promise you. They're tough boys."

There it was again. Ted had run his legs off on the play, and without a word of encouragement. Just an avowal that he had been "lucky."

The team scrimmaged every day after classes, and a few days later Ted had settled down to the routine and had learned the plays. The squad was composed of a bunch of nice, clean-cut fellows who were eager to put Midvale on the sports map, without a single gold brick among them.

Barbara Cromwell's brother Jim was second-string fullback, and he hit it off with Norman Macrae better than any of the others. But he seemed to resent Ted's place on the team, and Bill Stratton explained.

"Jim's a little peeved," he said, "because he figured he would be varsity if you weren't here. He's a good kid, but he can't play football as well as he thinks he can.

He gets along with the coach so well because Macrae is sweet on his sister."

"You're kidding," Ted said. "Why—Macrae's twenty-five!"

Bill Stratton laughed. "There aren't too many years between them. Heck, my dad's eleven years older than my mother!"

When Ted left the lockers that afternoon he went back to the campus and strolled around alone. He was still impressed by the rolling lawns, the full trees, and the sight of the squat buildings. In front of one of the buildings was a quaint well with a wooden bucket beside it, and he rested his arms on the edge of the well and peered down, watching the way the water sparkled like shining stars.

Suddenly there was a musical voice behind him. It said, "Hello, Mr. Ryan. Don't tell me you need the services of our wishing well!"

It was Barbara Cromwell, and Ted smiled at her. "Is that what this is—a wishing well?"

Barbara nodded pertly and came over to stand beside him, looking into the well. "They say that whatever you wish for here will come true, if you want it badly enough."

"Oh? How does it work?"

"Well," Barbara explained, "you toss a coin into the well, and then you look at the exact center of the ripples and make your wish."

Ted put a hand in his pocket. He said, "I'm going to give it a try," and dropped a coin.

After a moment of silence, Barbara said, "What did you wish for?"

Ted shook his head. "That's not fair. It wouldn't come true if I told."

"You're just afraid to tell me," Barbara chided. "I'll bet it's about a girl!"

Ted turned and looked at her. "I was wishing," he said quietly, "that you would let me walk home with you, and that on the way we could stop at the Sugar Bowl."

"Well," Barbara said hesitantly, "I certainly can't let our wishing well down. Here you are—Ted." And she handed him her books.

He waited for her again the following two afternoons, and suggested that they go to the movies the next night, which was Saturday.

"I'm sorry," Barbara said, "but I can't."

Ted felt his spirits drop. He said, "Another date?"

She nodded.

"I know it's none of my business," Ted said, "but is it with Norman Macrae?"

She said that it was, and Ted said "Oh" in a whisper.

"But I'm not doing anything Sunday," Barbara quickly suggested. "If you like, we could go for a walk or something."

Sunday came too slowly and went too quickly, and then it was Monday afternoon and more practice. They scrimmaged for a while and then, at Macrae's orders, the ball changed hands and the second-string tried to buck for yardage. On the third down, after being stopped dead for two, Jim Cromwell took the ball on a reverse. He had beautiful blocking and went through in a breeze; the play had caught the varsity eleven completely unawares.

Then the field was clear to the goal posts, with the exception of Walt Grayson and Ted. Grayson tried to nail young Cromwell but missed.

Ted judged the point where he would be able to intersect the line of the maroon-jerseyed runner, and started pumping his legs. Jim tried to dodge, but he was too close to the side lines to escape. Ted dived and hit him hard, just above the knees, and they went down together.

Ted rolled over and bounced to his feet, and as he did so he saw that Jim was holding his left arm painfully, his face contorted. He had tried to brace the fall, and a bone had snapped!

"Gosh, I'm sorry, Jim," said Ted, trying to help the lad to his feet. "I didn't think—"

"Take your hands off me," Jim snapped, shrugging Ted away. "I don't want any help from a professional athlete like you!"

And Norman Macrae was caustic, too. In the lockers, after Doc Stein had administered emergency treatment before taking Jim to the hospital, the coach said, "Well, Ryan, that fixes everything up just fine! Here I've been banking on having Cromwell in the secondary, and you put him out for the season."

"I couldn't help it, Coach," Ted tried to explain. "It was an accident. The way Jim fell—"

"Save your excuses," Macrae broke in. "You haven't

caused me anything but trouble since you first showed up at Midvale—and I'm telling you right now, you'd better make up for it on the field!"

But Professor John Cromwell was understanding, and when Ted made his explanations he said, "Things like that happen, my boy, and there is no use worrying about them. I'm just thankful it was his left arm, because it won't make him miss out on his studies. His future is so much more important than a lost season of football."

Ted waited for Barbara again that afternoon after scrimmage, and before she came out he dropped another coin into the wishing well and wished with all his might that she would not be angry.

But it seemed that the well had lost its mystic powers, for when she came through the swinging glass doors she marched straight down the steps onto the sidewalk without looking at him.

"Barbara!" he called and ran after her. "Wait a minute!"

"I'm not interested in anything you have to say, Ted Ryan," she said, holding her head stiff, her eyes straight ahead. "Norman Macrae and Jim both told me what happened."

"But it was all an accident," Ted argued. "If they said anything else they weren't telling the truth."

Barbara suddenly stopped and stared at him coldly. "Are you trying to say that Norman and my brother are liars?" she demanded. "I didn't think you would stoop so low!"

And then she took a tiny handkerchief from the patent leather belt around her waist and sobbed into it as she turned away and ran down the sidewalk.

Ted had an empty feeling in his stomach the rest of the week and he went through his studies and scrimmage periods mechanically. Then it was Saturday, the day of the opener against King College, and Norman Macrae was haranguing the team in the lockers.

"For two straight years Midvale has lost to King," he said. "But this time we're going to win—understand? We're going to win if I have to plan every play from the bench and send in a new quarterback every time the ball changes hands." He swept cold eyes over the players assembled before him, staring at each one individually. "I won't stand for inefficiency," he warned, "and anybody who doesn't make the grade will have a permanent reservation on the bench. Is that clear?"

Ted looked around at the boys and saw the way they were fidgeting under the tongue-lashing. And suddenly he knew that he had to speak up for them.

"You're not helping things very much, Coach," he said quietly. "The boys are nervous already, and you're making them worse."

"And who asked for your opinion?" snapped Macrae. "I'll have you know that I'm running this team, and that it will be run the way I want it."

"You're making a mistake," Ted said. "You can't win games that way."

Without moving his eyes from Ted, the coach said, "Adams!"

Will Adams said "Yes, sir" quickly.

"You replace Ryan in the starting line-up," Macrae ordered. "All right, now get out there—and remember, I won't have anything except high score!"

But the squad did not move. The boys looked at each other dourly, and then Bill Stratton said, "We'll need Ted in there, Coach. It's going to be a tough game."

Macrae's jaw dropped in surprise. He said tightly, "Are you turning rebel, too?"

"It's not that," Bill explained. "It's just—"

"Nelson," roared Macrae, his face white, "start at left half for Stratton." Then he said, "Any others?"

There were none, and the team filed out to the field. A great yell went up from the Midvale cheering section, but there was not a single man on the squad who thought they would be able to live up to the faith the school was putting in them.

On the bench, Ted and Bill watched glumly as Midvale took the toss and elected to receive. Ted said, "Thanks for standing up for me, but you shouldn't have done it. You just got yourself tossed out, too."

The big blond halfback said, "Forget it. I don't care for myself, but you're on scholarship. I'm afraid Macrae will try to get it rescinded."

Ted wasn't sure what the word meant, but he didn't like the way it sounded. And then came the kickoff, and there was no time to think about his own problems.

Walt Grayson took the ball on the twenty-yard-line and tucked it away. He cut straight down the field

toward the charging orange and black team, trying to
follow his interference. A speedy King man spilled him
on the thirty-two.

They huddled, and then Jesse Nelson took it and
tried to plunge off-tackle, but he was stopped for no
gain. They hit the other side of the line on the next
down, feeling them out, and Nelson was thrown back
two yards. The third was a spinner which picked up
about three yards around right end, and then they
kicked out and King brought it to their own forty-one.

The game seesawed back and forth at mid-field with
neither team gaining much of an advantage, and then
Jolly Wordell, the King coach, sent in a new quarterback and things began to happen.

They heaved a short pass that was good for eight
yards on the second down, and then powerhoused
through the middle of the Midvale line for the other
two. The King boys were suddenly clicking, and at the
end of the period they were down to Midvale's twelve-
yard-line.

On the side lines, Norman Macrae was ranting and
raving. "Numbskulls! Idiots! Morons!" he exclaimed.
"They're throwing the game, and I won't have it!" He
ran cold eyes over the bench, skipping Ted and Bill,
and snapped, "Michals—Dobbins—Stokes—House. Get
in there, and hold them. Understand? Hold them!"

The four guards and tackles grabbed up their hel-
mets and raced out to the field, and Ted said to Bill,
"Nice way to run a team. Beat them over the head
with a baseball bat."

The ball changed to the other end of the field and

King tried to push it over. But the reinforced Midvale line held—for the moment, anyway. When King got the ball again they bucked once and then pulled a spectacular pass that Will Adams should have stopped, and the fans went wild as the referee threw up his hands to signify a touchdown.

The conversion kick was blocked by Bert Sharp, and Midvale went back to receive again. On the bench, Ted watched anxiously as Walt Grayson snagged the ball and pumped to the thirty-eight. The boys played hard for the remainder of the period, but they were not able to put it over. If it was any consolation, King barged down to the fifteen again and could not score, though they tried everything in the books.

In the lockers at the half Norman Macrae raged at his battered players, ending with the usual tirade to which Ted had now become accustomed.

"I will not stand for inefficiency," he warned them again. "You played that first half like a bunch of ragged school kids, and I'm ashamed to call you my team. I want two touchdowns this half. Understand—*two!* And I want the plays run that I call. From the stupidity I saw out there, there's not a player among you that I can trust to call them right."

Ernie Prentiss said, "How about putting Stratton and Ryan back in, Coach? We can use them plenty."

Macrae did not like to go back on his orders, and he deliberated a moment. Then he said, "All right— Stratton, you go in this half, and make it good or I'll pull you again."

Bill said, "What about Ted?"

"He stays on the bench," Macrae barked. "He needs the discipline."

"Then so do I," Bill said simply. "He goes in with me, or I stay out with him."

"Then you both stay out," the coach said without hesitation, "and I'll see that Dean Monks hears about this little mutiny. I'll get action if it's the last thing I do!"

As they returned to the bench, Bill said, "I'm sorry, Ted. I thought I was doing the right thing, but all I did was get you in deeper."

Ted tried to smile, but he was hardly in the mood. "Forget it," he said. "I want you to know that I appreciate everything."

Midvale received again and the game went along the third quarter without much excitement, even with the numerous instruction-carrying substitutes Macrae sent in. Then the field changed for the last time and Ted couldn't stand it any longer. The boys out there were getting visibly weaker, and he was burning with desire to get into the game.

He jumped from the bench and went up to Norman Macrae just as Will Adams punted out of danger from the twenty.

"Get in there for Prentiss," Macrae was yelling to Joe Bailey. "Throw passes when you get the ball—and make them good. I want a touchdown, and quick!" Then Bailey ran out to the field and the coach looked coldly at Ted and said, "What do you want, Ryan?"

"I want to get out there and play ball," Ted said. "Haven't you kept me on the bench long enough?"

"Get back where you belong," Macrae grated. "I'm still running this team."

"Look," Ted said quietly. "You don't like me and I don't like you. O.K. That's a personal problem. But Midvale isn't personal. We've got to work together whether we like it or not, and the school needs this game."

Macrae's face was a mask for a long second, and then he said, "All right, go ahead in. But it's for the school, Ryan, I want you to remember that."

"Yes, sir," Ted said and grinned. "What about Bill Stratton?"

Macrae waved his hand in annoyance. "He goes, too. Nelson's just about fagged out, anyway. But get this, Ryan," he added in a hard voice. "I want passes out there. Pass them silly, and then throw more passes. It's the only way to pull this one out of the fire. Now get going!" And then came the dig. "We're paying you to play football, so see if you can earn your keep."

Ted and Bill rushed out there and Nelson and Adams came back. It was King's ball on Midvale's thirty-five, third down and three to go.

"O.K., boys," Ted said to the tired team, talking it up. "Let's hold 'em for old Midvale, and the heck with Macrae. Knock those guys down!" He backtracked to the safety slot as the King center left the huddle.

Signals were called and the ball went back. It was easy to see the play forming—right down the middle. The burly King line opened a hole and pushed, and their halfback charged into it. But Bill Stratton was

there at the same time and sent him tumbling back
again.

King went into punt formation and Ted went down
the field to receive. The kick was high and slow, and
he was pulled down almost as soon as the ball hit his
hands.

"The coach wants passes," Ted said as they went
back to huddle. "On your toes!"

Joe Bailey called the play and Ted took the snap-
back. He faked a run to the left, suddenly pivoted, and
let one go to Les McBride on the other side of the field.
It was right in McBride's hands and he couldn't have
missed it, but somehow he did. The ball was grounded
for an incompletion.

"Another one?" Joe Bailey said in the huddle.
"Might be risky."

"Let's see what happens," Bill Stratton suggested.
"We can't miss them all."

Ted took the ball and faded. He looked around for
receivers, but they had been blanketed and there was
nothing to do but run. Walt Grayson saw the predica-
ment and blocked, knocking down a King end and
then scrambling up again.

Ted tucked the ball under his arm and charged to
the far side of the field. The King backs went with
him, and he cut sharply to the inside, just eluding a
tackler. Then he was in the midst of them and fighting
for yardage. A pair of strong arms went around his
waist and he twisted and squirmed to shake the man
off and plunge ahead. For a few seconds it was a crazy
turmoil, and then the Midvale boys rallied to his de-

fense and cut down the opposition. The field was suddenly clear, with the exception of the safety man.

Ted streaked down the field, his heart singing above the excited screams from the stands. He angled over to the sideline, his feet just inches from the chalk.

Then the King man was on him, and Ted threw out a stiff arm and dug in as he pivoted. His hand caught the tackler on the side of the helmet and pushed him away, and Ted crossed the final stripe on his feet!

The Midvale fans went raving mad. The horns started blowing, the drums banging, and above it all was the college victory yell. The score was now tied up at 6–6, and they wanted that extra point.

The squad was jubilant as it went back to huddle, but then the boys quieted and Joe Bailey said, "Another aerial?"

"Try a sneak," Ted suggested in a whisper. "You take it."

The old play still worked, and Bailey went across for the extra point.

The team from King fought hard after that, but it was no use. Midvale held, and though they did not score again, the game had been won.

But if Norman Macrae was happy about the outcome he certainly did not show it. In the lockers he said, "Luck, luck, luck—that's all it was. You played as if you were having a pillow fight out there. But I'll change that all right! From now on you'll really work at scrimmage. I'll make football players out of you if I have to kill you doing it!"

Ted said, "Look, Coach, you got your win and the boys are tired. Get off their necks for once."

Norman Macrae's lips twitched and his eyes hardened. "Are you still looking for trouble, Ryan?" he challenged. "If you are, I'll see that you get it!"

Ted shook his head. "No," he said, "I don't want any trouble. All I want is to be treated like a human being. That's all any of us want. Maybe it was only seven to six, but we won the game—the first time Midvale has licked King in three years."

Macrae seemed apoplectic for a moment, but he quickly gained control of himself. He knew he had pushed the team too far, that they were behind Ted, and that if he pressed the matter there might be a serious showdown. But still he could not backtrack. That would have been a sign of weakness, and Norman Macrae was a strong-willed man if nothing else.

He said brusquely, "Then we'll forget about the King game. There won't be another mention of it in the lockers. But you can take my word for it that we're going to win the others with higher scores!"

It was a psychological victory for Ted, but one that gave him no satisfaction. He would have preferred the kind of harmony that should exist between a coach and his team, and he felt that everybody would have benefited from such a relation.

The season wore on and Midvale continued to be successful, whether by ability or the luck which Norman Macrae insisted. And though Ted made touchdowns on the field, he was not able to come any closer to Barbara Cromwell. She deliberately avoided him, and when he did run into her at the Sugar Bowl or at the Strand Theatre, she was always in the company of Norman Macrae.

He bumped into her once by accident, while bicycling on Old Country Road, but the experience was unpleasant and Ted preferred to forget it.

She was hiking and wearing slacks and a leather jacket against the cool autumn winds, and Ted quickly rode up to her and jumped from his bike, walking it along.

He said, "I—I've been wanting to see you, Barbara. I've missed you a lot."

"You have?" she said stiffly.

"Yes. I thought—I've hoped that we could patch things up."

"There's nothing to patch up," she told him. "That was a mean thing to do, just so you could protect your scholarship."

"But it was an accident," Ted pleaded. "Gosh, I didn't mean to break Jim's arm!"

Barbara said, "Do you expect me to believe that?"

"Certainly I do!" Ted exclaimed. "I don't dislike anybody enough to want to hurt him."

Barbara said, "What about Norman Macrae? He told me you deliberately turned the team against him. That's hurting somebody, isn't it?"

"If Macrae said that, he's not telling the truth," Ted answered hotly. "He's nothing but a bully, and nobody likes him."

"Jim likes him," Barbara insisted. "And so do I. But Jim doesn't like you, and neither does Norman."

Ted murmured, "What about you?"

The girl was silent for perhaps twenty yards, and then she said falteringly, "I thought I liked you— once." Her voice became stronger as she added, "But now it's different, and I wish you would leave me alone!"

Then it was time for the mid-term examinations. Ted felt that he would be able to pass them all without trouble, with the sole exception of chemistry. He had spent long hours trying to master the various formulas, but some of them still confused him.

The test was not nearly as bad as he had expected, though, and his pen flew over the printed forms as he sat in the silent chemistry lab with the other students under the watchful eye of Professor Cromwell.

"How was it?" the amiable professor inquired, as Ted came up to the desk and handed in his paper. "Difficult?"

"Not too hard, Professor," Ted whispered. "I was afraid of it at first, but I think I passed." He corrected himself, "I *know* I passed."

Professor Cromwell smiled. "Well, we'll see, my boy, we'll see. I'll keep my fingers crossed for you. It will be too bad if your marks keep you out of the game against State next week."

Ted kept his fingers crossed, too. State was Midvale's traditional rival, and this year the larger college had trounced all opposition without having a single point scored against it. It had an entirely new backfield of juniors who had been groomed during the sophomore and freshman years. One of these boys—Percy Kane, a gorilla of a fullback who belied his name—had already received offers from the pro clubs. It was rumored that he had signed up with the Yanks, but there was neither confirmation nor denial from Kane or the New York outfit.

It was the following Tuesday when the bombshell struck. Chemistry was Ted's last class of the day and he had tried to understand Professor Cromwell's talk on halogens. At the end of the talk the professor removed his pince-nez bifocals and smiled at the class.

"Well, ladies and gentlemen," he announced, "tomorrow is the big day. I expect to finish grading papers tonight, and I think you might like to know that they have been much better than I expected. Your marks will be posted tomorrow."

Excited murmurs ran through the class and Professor Cromwell looked at the electric wall clock. "That will be all for today," he said. "Oh—er—Mr. Ryan, will you remain a minute, please?"

The students filed out and Ted went up to the professor's desk. "Yes, sir," he said. "Did I do something wrong?"

Professor Cromwell cleared his throat and pinched the glasses back on his nose. He said, "It's about your test, Ted. I thought I'd better tell you."

Ted smiled. "Oh, I knew I passed all right, Professor. It wasn't too bad."

Professor Cromwell frowned over his glasses. "That's

just it, my boy," he said slowly. "I can't understand it. I can't understand it at all. You failed miserably—even on the simple questions."

"But that's impossible!" Ted cried. "I passed the test! I *know* I did!"

The professor shook his head sadly. "I'm sorry, Ted," he sympathized. "Truly I am. But I'll have to inform Mr. Macrae that you will not be eligible for sports participation the remainder of this term."

It hit Ted with the force of a solid straight-arm, and he left the chemistry lab in a daze. Everything had gone against him, leaving no possible way to escape. First it had been Jim Cromwell, then Barbara, and now the professor. All his troubles seemed to have the Cromwells mixed up in them somewhere.

He felt the urge to rush out and catch the next train home, but he knew that his father would not approve. He would have to stay and face it and take what was coming to him. That was the only way his father would want it.

The squad was sympathetic the next day when he went to the lockers to get some of his things.

"We'll miss you a lot in there, Ted," said Blimp Friedman, the big guard. "It'll be tough to push them over without you."

"I can't understand it," Ernie Prentiss said, puzzled. "You said it was such an easy exam."

"Why don't you check with Professor Cromwell?" suggested Bill Stratton. "Maybe he made a mistake."

But Norman Macrae was vitriolic. He said, "It seems that other people won't stand for inefficiency either,

Ryan. I told you you were heading for trouble—and you've messed up my backfield to boot. Now I'll really have a job against State!"

It was typical of what Ted had expected from the coach. Macrae was so self-centered that he didn't care about anything except himself and *his* game. He probably even figured that Ted had failed the examination just to get even with him!

Thursday and Friday came and went, and then it was the day of the game. The skies were cloudy and the prediction was rain, but all of Midvale had turned out for the traditional battle in spite of the weather, and right now the stands were packed, waiting for the kickoff.

But Ted had no stomach for football. He was lying face-down on his dormitory cot, trying to shut out the sounds coming from the stands, when suddenly he got an idea and quickly jumped to his feet, his eyes flashing hopefully.

He ran down the stairs, threw open the dormitory door and left it open, and sprinted across the campus as fast as his legs would take him. His heart was thumping wildly, and he prayed with all his might that Professor Cromwell would be in the chemistry lab.

He was, and when Ted rushed in he said in surprise, "Why, Ted! What are you doing here?"

"Professor," Ted said breathlessly, "I have an idea. Do you still have my examination papers?"

Cromwell nodded, his brow furrowed. "Yes, I have them here in my desk. Why, what is this all about?"

"Good!" Ted cried, his excitement rising. "I've been

thinking about it, Professor, and the more I think the more I can't understand how I flunked."

The professor said quietly, "Are you doubting my marking of your papers, Ted?"

"Oh, no, sir!" Ted exclaimed. "But I wonder if you would ask me some of the questions right now, and see how I do on them?"

Professor Cromwell pulled on his lower lip and said: "H'mm. It's unorthodox and I don't see what you have to gain, but I'll do it. . . . What is Avogadro's Law?"

Ted rattled it off without hesitation. "Equal volumes of gases, provided they are measured under the same conditions as to temperature and pressure, contain the same number of molecules."

The professor said "H'mm" again. Then, "Under what conditions do chlorine and hydrogen best combine?"

"Direct sunlight. They will not combine at all in the dark."

The professor shook his head. "That's strange, Ted," he puzzled. "You got both of those questions wrong on the test." He opened a desk drawer and in a moment came up with a sheaf of papers. "Look for yourself."

Ted looked, and as he looked he gasped. "Professor!" he shouted, "That's not my handwriting! I never turned in these papers!"

The professor's brows knitted and he said, "Here, let me see," and took the test sheets. The frown deepened to a scowl as he studied the printed forms, and he said, "You're absolutely correct. I'm going to look into this right away!"

"Then I'll be able to play?" Ted said anxiously.

Professor Cromwell got up from behind his desk and walked hurriedly toward the door, carrying the test papers. "We'll see," he said sternly. "Come with me."

As they left the building young Jim Cromwell, his arm in a sling, was climbing the steps. He said, "Dad— wait. I want to talk to you."

"No time now," the professor said brusquely. "See me later."

C329764 CO. SCHOOLS

"But, Dad," Jim called. "It's important."

"Later!" his father commanded and kept going. "I have to see the dean."

Ted followed the professor to the stadium, and just as they went through the gates the crowd roared and his heart dropped. It was the kickoff, with State receiving.

The professor led the way through the jammed stands, and Ted had no time to watch the game. Then they were at the faculty box and Professor Cromwell spoke earnestly to the portly prexy of Midvale, Archibald Monks. Ted could not hear what was being said because of the noise of the crowd, but he wasn't trying to listen. Barbara Cromwell was in the box, two rows above Dean Monks, and he was looking at her.

Then Professor Cromwell said, "Ted!" The latter tore his eyes from the girl and answered, "Yes, sir."

"This is a serious matter, young man," Dean Monks said solemnly. "Very serious. It is a reflection on the integrity of the school to have such a thing occur."

Ted said, "Yes, sir," and the dean went on: "You will be given another opportunity to take the examination, of course. But since you are not on the records as having officially passed, I'm afraid that you will not be eligible for this game."

"But, sir," Ted tried to object. "This is our biggest game! They might need—"

"I'm sorry," the dean interrupted. "Very sorry."

Ted suddenly got another idea, and he said anxiously, "Then why not let me take the test right here? Professor Cromwell has the questions, and all he has to do is ask them!"

The two faculty members looked at each other with raised eyebrows, and Dean Monks shook his head. "I'm sorry," he said bluntly, "but Midvale is a school of learning, not a—"

"Come, now, Arch," Professor Cromwell entreated. "Don't be the high and mighty dean today. Let's give the boy a break."

Dean Monks looked stern for a moment, and then he started to chuckle in delight. The chuckle rose in volume to a deep laugh that made his stuffed waistline bounce, and he said, "All right, go ahead. But I must say that it's the first time in history an examination has been given in a stadium during a football game!"

So Professor Cromwell and Ted went to work, and the game progressed out on the field.

Sometime during the second quarter a deafening yell went up from the State stands on the other side of the field, followed by low moans from the Midvale students, and Ted knew that State had scored. He redoubled his efforts, rushing his answers to Professor Cromwell's questions.

There was only one more page to go after the half-time bands had paraded and the teams came back to the field. And then, at last, Professor Cromwell asked the final question and Ted rattled off the answer and sighed.

"How did I do, Professor?" he asked, after taking a quick look at the field, and seeing State down on the Midvale twenty.

"Just a minute," Professor Cromwell answered. "I haven't finished."

Ted's heart raced as he waited, and then the professor smiled. "It's all right, my boy," he said. "You can get into your suit. I'll tell Coach Macrae," he added, but Ted did not hear him. He was already fighting through the crowd to the lockers.

He changed with nervous fingers, leaving his clothes where they fell, and as he slipped into the shoulder pads another yell went up from the stands. By its intensity he knew that it meant another touchdown, but not for Midvale.

Then, with his shoes still untied and his jersey tail out, he ran to the bench. Midvale had the ball and Norman Macrae was going crazy, pacing up and down on the side lines. When he saw Ted he barked, "It's about time, Ryan! Get out there and earn your keep!"

The boys were glad to see Ted, and Bill Stratton slapped him on the back and said, "What happened, fella? How come they let you in?"

"You gave me the idea," Ted told him. "Cromwell made a mistake on the papers."

"Now let's make up for lost time," Walt Grayson put in hurriedly. "That Percy Kane guy is really a tough cookie!"

They huddled and Ernie Prentiss whispered, "Their left wing is murder, Ted. Stay away from it. Make it nineteen on six. Let's go!"

Hank Smith got down over the ball and the line formed on him. Ernie Prentiss called the signals, and Ted shifted to receive. It came back on six and he was running before it touched his fingers, slicing hard to plunge through the end-tackle gap that he knew would be open when he got there.

He went through for three yards, and then a scythe cut his legs from under him and threw him to the ground with a thud. Percy Kane had made the tackle, and he was grinning when they got up.

"That's far enough today, hurry boy," Kane said in a booming voice that went with his barrel chest. "You come through, I'll slice you down."

"I see what you mean," Ted told Walt Grayson as they went back. "I didn't even see Kane coming."

"Time to kick again," Prentiss said tiredly. "Boot it out, Ted, on seven."

They went into punt formation and State moved back. Ted flexed his toes and held out his hands, and as he did so he suddenly decided that he was going to run instead. He had been able to get through the State line on the previous play, and Midvale needed only four more yards for a first down. Besides, Kane had pulled back to receive.

Les McBride and Bert Sharp bumped the State ends

and then got out there, while Walt Grayson and Bill Stratton blocked. They didn't know Ted's plans, but they did their work effectively.

At the same time, Ted was digging in, swinging wide around the left end. He picked up eight yards and brought the Midvale fans roaring to their feet before Kane bulldozed in and smashed him down again.

"Thought you'd pull a fast one, huh?" Kane bellowed. "Well, I'll watch you, sweetheart!"

When they huddled again Ernie Prentiss said, "That was crazy!" but his eyes were smiling. "Let's make it twenty-three on this one."

The ball came back and Ted gave it to Walt Grayson on a spinner, and the halfback took it around the end for two yards. The next play Bill Stratton dropped a yard, and then Ted punted out.

Percy Kane took it, and he had the strength of two men. He straight-armed Bert Sharp out of the way and dragged Larry Hall and Les McBride three yards before they downed him.

Kane took it again on the play and shouldered his way through the forward wall. Ernie Prentiss hit him low and hung on, but he stayed on his feet and picked up another yard before Ted dived in and toppled him.

"There's one for you," Ted told the big fullback, grinning. "Midvale style."

Kane scowled and went back to huddle, and as they came up to the ball again the dark skies rumbled and rain started coming down. In only seconds it was a drenching torrent and loud squeals came from the stands.

Ted came in a few yards, knowing that with a slippery ball State would not pass. Then Kane got it and was running into the hole his powerful line was opening. But Ted was there to close it, and he clamped onto the runner and held tight.

Suddenly the ball slithered from Kane's fingers and there was a mad scramble. The players heaped up, and when the referee scattered them Blimp Friedman was on bottom—the ball held tightly beneath him!

Ted thumped the big guard on the back and yelled: "Nice going, fella! Now we roll!"

Blimp grunted and said, "Sure, but which way? In this rain it'll be more like swimming."

Ted frowned. The Midvale boys thought they had lost the game already, and that was not good. It added another strike to the one they already had against them. He motioned to Ernie Prentiss to call time, and as they lay on the sopping grass with the rain beating at them he said:

"Look, guys, this Percy Kane is only human. He laces his shoes the same way we do, and we can stop him if we want to."

Larry Hall said, "With what? We've tried all the tricks, and he still comes through."

But Bill Stratton agreed with Ted. He said, "Are you going to give up to State that easy? Let's show them that Midvale has more than just the prettiest girls in the country!"

Ted let them think about it, and then time was called in and they went back to huddle. Ernie Prentiss said, "Make it thirty-one, on three."

"Wait a minute," Ted suggested. "How about a pass? They'll never expect it!"

Prentiss scowled. "Will you be able to throw the ball in this rain?"

Ted said grimly, "I'll throw it, if the ends can catch it."

Walt Grayson took the ball and shuffle-passed it back to Ted as Bill Stratton faked an end-around. Ted took the slippery ball and ran toward the side lines, looking for a receiver. And then Les McBride was in the clear, way down in the end zone, and Ted dug his fingers into the seams and let it go into the rain. He knew that it was Midvale's big chance to score, that if Les McBride missed, the team would lose spirits for sure.

And then he was yelling, his voice drowned out by the terrific earsplitting screams mushrooming from the stands. Les had somehow caught the ball!

The frenzy of the Midvale fans increased when Bill Stratton took it across the mud for the extra point. State's seven-point lead was not so large now, and the touchdown seemed to give the Midvale boys just the spark they needed.

Ted's scoring pass was the last play of the quarter, and Walt Grayson kicked a flat spinner when they changed the field.

The ball splashed crazily along the ground, bouncing and jumping like a thing alive. Percy Kane got it in his hands and it popped out. Then he was on it again. But Bert Sharp was in there, too, and he made the tackle before the halfback could move an inch.

"Hey! He's not so tough after all," Bert announced

when he came back. "All you've got to do is slam it into him."

"That's what I tried to tell you," Ted said. "O.K., now let's hold them!"

The Midvale line became solid, and State was forced to kick out after losing four yards. Ted was back to receive the treacherous ball. It was coated and muddy and hard to hold, but he wrapped both arms around it and dug in. A State tackler dropped him on the thirty-two, and the ball squished from his grasp. There was another mad scramble, but the referee had already blown his whistle.

It was impossible to try any fancy ball handling in the chilling downpour, so they just kept hitting the line. After picking up seven yards Ernie Prentiss called for a punt. Ted went back and took it, but Bert Sharp did not bump his man solidly enough and he was in in a flash, trying to block the kick.

Ted saw the player coming and quickly toed the ball. But he was not soon enough, and it hit the top of the State man's head and bounced to the side.

It was a free ball, and Ted scooped it up hurriedly and splashed down the field. Most of the State players were on the ground, and the others did not know what was happening. In the confusion Ted got down to the ten before Percy Kane woke up and came after him.

Ted put out a stiff arm and caught the big man on the chin, but still he came on. The tackle was too high to cut Ted's legs from under him, and he dug in with renewed strength, dragging Kane with him. Then the

State man dropped his arms lower and Ted went down. But Kane had not been soon enough. The ball was across the line!

"There's another one," Ted said to Kane above the din from the stands. "What's the matter—your scythe worn out?"

The big fullback growled under his breath. "It's not over yet, brother," he said. "Just try and make that extra point!"

They tried, but it was no good. Bill Stratton took the ball for an end-around, but he didn't even reach the scrimmage line. Percy Kane was in there, and he hit the Midvale boy so hard he drove him back a full ten yards.

"What happens now?" Ernie Prentiss asked as they trotted back to kick. "That one-point lead is still enough for them to win."

"We wait for a break," Ted said. "Don't worry, it'll come."

But it did not come. The State team wasn't taking any chances, and they stalled until the referee penalized them for delaying the game. And Midvale was held tight on the ground, with only short gains.

Time was running out, and when there were only two and a half minutes remaining in the game Ernie Prentiss said, "When do we get that break? If it's coming, it better come darn quick!"

"It'll come," Ted said with an assurance he did not feel. "Just you wait and see."

State kicked out and Bill Stratton got the ball. He

ran toward the side lines and Ted went with him to block. Suddenly a State player came from nowhere and Ted knew he would not be able to stop him.

"Lateral, Bill!" he shouted. "Quick!"

The blond halfback tossed the ball just as the orange and blue tackler hit him. It juggled on the tips of Ted's fingers for a heart-stopping second, and then he had it and was streaking away. Percy Kane came over and knocked him out of bounds on the twenty-one.

"There's part of your break," Ted said, grinning, as they went back. "Now let's keep going!"

Walt Grayson made three yards on a mud-sloppy spinner, Bill Stratton picked up four more on a line plunge, and then Ted was thrown for a two-yard loss to put them down on the sixteen-yard-line.

"Too far to go," Ernie Prentiss said, shaking his head. "We'll never make it."

"Amen!" Walt Grayson added. "It's the ball game."

"We can try a field goal," Ted suggested hopefully. "How about it, Ernie?"

They all thought it was crazy. The distance was not too great, but the angle was bad, and the ball was waterlogged. But Prentiss said, "Go ahead. Might as well try it."

Ted's nerves were tight as he shifted into the slot. He looked at the goal posts through the rain, and shuddered. If he had only thought of it sooner they could have worked the ball over. If only—

And then the ball was in his hands and his heart stopped. He looked at the goal posts again, then dropped the ball as he hopped on his left foot and brought the right one back

His toes squished in sopping shoes as the foot met the ball, and then he closed his eyes. This was it. Good or bad, it was Midvale's last chance.

There was a long moment of silence, and then a roar from the stands blasted in Ted's ears. It was good! The ball had somehow slipped between those narrow crossbars!

The Midvale boys were suddenly around Ted, beating him on the back and screaming in his ears. They were deliriously happy, the ball game be hanged.

"Wait'll we get in the lockers!" Ernie Prentiss said, laughing. "Macrae will call it the greatest piece of luck in football history!"

The rest of the game was anticlimactical, and State had the ball for only three downs, in which they weren't able to move a yard against Midvale opposition. And then they were going in, the victors by two points!

Professor Cromwell, Barbara, and young Jim Cromwell, looking downcast, were at the locker doors when Ted ran up. The professor stopped him with a hand on his arm and drew him aside.

"Fine game, my boy," he said. "Fine game! But"—his voice broke—"I thought you would like to know, I found the . . . I found who had—had meddled. It was—it was my own son," he confessed in a whisper.

Jim Cromwell said quietly, "I—I'm sorry, Ted. I—I tried to tell Dad before, but he wouldn't listen."

"Jim owned up," the professor said, the muscles of his face taut with the shame and misery he felt. "He came up to me right after you went into the game, and told me he had switched papers."

Suddenly it was all clear to Ted, and he smiled. "Well, I don't blame you, Jim," he said. He put out a hand. "What do you say, fella? Let's shake and forget about it. O.K.?"

Jim Cromwell hesitated briefly, and then he took Ted's hand. And Ted was glad. He knew that he had made a good friendship, one that would last.

Then something happened that made him blush right down to his muddy shoes. Barbara threw her arms around his neck and kissed him on the cheek through all the mud.

Ted said "Gosh!" breathlessly. "Gosh, Barbara!"

To anyone else the girl would have looked funny, with that smear of mud around her smiling mouth. But to Ted she was beautiful, and as she backed away she whispered, "I'll wait for you, Ted. . . . At the wishing well."

Ted turned to rush into the lockers, and saw that Norman Macrae was at the door, watching it all. The coach was scowling darkly, and as Ted pushed past him he said, "Humph! Puppy love!"

The Star-Dust Kid

EVEN NOW, as he stepped through the door and into the Bruins' locker room, Phil Johnson could not believe that it was all true. He was officially a member of the baseball club he had always followed so avidly—signed, sealed, and now delivered—but he still could not understand how it had happened. Only a week before he had been playing sand-lot baseball, and now, suddenly, he was in the big league.

He stood there, big, black-haired, and gawky, and swept his eyes wide with amazement about the talking and laughing bunch. There was Bernie Wilson, the hefty first-sacker, putting a stick of chewing gum into his big mouth. Rawboned Joe Haslip, the short fielder, with a pillow in one hand and a streak of greased lightning in the other. Powerful Lew Prescott and gangling Hal Adams, the greatest pair of power-punchers in the league. And there, against the wall, struggling into his uniform decorated with a blazing "B," was Charley Double, the veteran hurler, who had been Phil's personal hero for as long as he could remember.

He felt like a kid in baseball's hall of fame, and a scared kid at that. He didn't know how these eagle-eyed men would take to him. Especially since he had been told that he was being signed up as a possible successor to the great Charley Double, who had trod the mound rubber for almost half of Phil's twenty-two years.

Stu Bacon, the pudgy and pugnacious backstop, was the first to see Phil. He smiled crookedly and yelled, "Hey, guys, look what the wind blew in. The hayseed, in person!"

The locker room was suddenly stilled, and Phil's face burned in embarrassment as all eyes turned toward him. He felt that they were giving him the once-over, making snap decisions as to whether he was Bruin material.

Then somebody moaned, "Our troubles are over. Now we've got a fireball pitcher!"

Somebody else said, "What does he use those big ears for—blinders, so he can't see the runners?"

And another voice, "Take it away! What did we ever do to deserve such an awful fate?"

Phil shifted uncomfortably from one foot to the other. He didn't know what to do. Were they serious, or were they just giving him the usual razzing? He couldn't tell from their faces.

"All right, break it up," Charley Double boomed from the other end of the room. "Give the kid a break." He dropped his pants to the bench and came over to Phil, a wide grin on his tanned, friendly face. "Welcome to the Bruins," he said and stuck out a big hand. "Don't let these bums throw you, they're just clowning."

Phil tried to return the grin. Maybe they were clowning and maybe they weren't. But he took the hand, and as it pressed into his a chill ran down his back. He was actually shaking the hand that had piloted the Bruins to a half dozen pennants, and that was worth all the ribbing in the world!

"Th-thank you, sir," he stammered. "I—"

"The name's Charley to you," Double said. "You don't say 'sir' to anybody around here except Bud Fraser."

Phil had already met Bud Fraser, the Bruins' owner. That had been only the previous week, in his home town of Northport. He had just finished pitching a shutout sand-lot game against the Tarrytown Tigers, the team from the next village down the road, when Fraser approached him.

"Fine game, young fellow," he had said. "You've got a good pitching arm there."

"You should have seen him against the Lanterns last week," Phil's young brother Hack piped up. "Those guys had to use radar to find the ball!"

"I did see him," Fraser said. "I saw the game before that too." He cleared his throat and went on, "Ever think of playing baseball professionally, young man? I mean, do you have that much interest in it?"

"Are you kidding, mister?" Phil had said. "I'd give my right arm to play for the pros."

That's when Fraser introduced himself. "I've been staying at the Van Wyck place on vacation," he said. "They told me you had the best pitching arm in the state, and I thought perhaps I could combine a bit of business with the pleasure. How would you like to pitch for the Bruins?"

The rest of that day was a blur. Phil remembered

something about money being discussed, and a waiver to protect the club if he didn't work out as expected. But that was all that registered—except that he would be tried out as replacement for Charley Double, whose arm was beginning to suffer from too many seasons on the mound.

And now he was in the locker room of the famed Bruins, and Charley Double, the greatest pitcher who had ever toed the rubber, had an arm around his shoulder and was saying, "Come on, Phil, and meet the boys."

They covered the entire roster, and though the fellows all seemed friendly enough, Phil thought he could sense a slight undercurrent of resentment. But he tried to tell himself that it was all imagination, that he was just expecting too much.

"Well, that's the bunch," Double said. "What do you think of them, son?"

"The best in baseball," Phil said. "I hope I'll be able to measure up to them."

"It'll take more than hoping, kid," Lew Prescott said in a lazy drawl. "The first thing you've got to do is get the star dust out of your eyes and learn that it takes more than an arm to be a pitcher."

"Yeah," Stu Bacon put in. "You've got to have a head on your shoulders and diamond savvy and a good front. If you've got all that, plus enough stuff to tag onto one now and then, it doesn't hurt to have a good arm."

"O.K., boys," Charley Double said to the team, "let's button it and hop out to the field. We've got a hot session ahead." And to Phil he added, "Vic Marshall's not here yet, so I'll dig out a suit for you." He walked around the corner to the stock room, the long tail of his shirt flapping crazily against the backs of his strong, slightly bowed legs.

When he returned he had a big grin plastered across his face and a uniform in his arms. "I hope you're not superstitious," he said, tossing the outfit to Phil. "It's the only one I could find, and the number is thirteen. Will that be O.K.?"

Later, as Phil pushed his feet into his cleated shoes, another Bruin came into the lockers. The top one of them all: the flaming-haired Vic Marshall, the playing manager who held down the keystone sack. And Marshall didn't make Phil feel any better.

He said, "You're Phil Johnson, aren't you?" And after Phil said that he was, Marshall went on bluntly, "Well, I want you to know how I feel about all this. I'll give you every chance to make good, but don't expect any backslapping unless you earn it."

"Yes, sir," Phil said quietly.

"As far as I'm concerned," Marshall went on, "my pitching staff is complete. I didn't ask Bud Fraser to sign you up, and unless you make good I'll recommend that you go on the block."

Phil smiled tightly, but the corners of his mouth quivered nervously.

He felt a little better when he got out on the mound and held the horsehide sphere in his hand. He threw a few in to Beef Burnham, one of the relief backstops, and some of his confidence returned. He tossed floaters, drops, and hooks until his arm was loose and well lubricated, and then Lew Prescott stepped up to the plate and stuck out a bat as big as the side of a barn.

"Put one across, kid," the slugger yelled, "and I'll drive you out of the park. Let's make it a quick trip!"

Stu Bacon, standing on the side lines, laughed raucously. "Let him toss a couple first, Lew," he taunted. "Then he can tell his hayseed friends he pitched for the Bruins. It'll make him a big shot!"

That started Phil's blood boiling. Maybe they didn't want him on the team. That was O.K. But there was no reason to make with the wise talk about his Northport friends. He wasn't going to take that from anybody.

He went into his wind-up and all the bitterness that had welled up within him exploded. He'd show them how a hayseed could lay them across the line!

The ball left the tips of his fingers at the end of a wide side-arm motion. It rocketed straight for Prescott's powerful frame, then broke at the last moment and scorched across the inside edge of the plate.

But Prescott had not waited. He hit the dirt and came up yelling as the ball thudded into Beef Burnham's glove.

"You crazy galoot!" he screamed. "You trying to kill me? Keep them down the middle where they belong!"

Vic Marshall was backing up Beef Burnham, watching them break. He said, "It was in there, Lew. Waist-high, across the inside. It would have been a called strike."

The slugger grumbled something to himself and picked up a handful of dirt. He rubbed the bat down and crowded the plate, eyes squinted to slits under his peaked cap.

Phil's lips split in a wide grin. He had struck pay dirt on his first pitch, and it made him feel better. Heck, he thought, these guys aren't so tough after all. They're just like the Tarrytown bunch, only a little bigger!

Beef got down in a crouch again and stuck his glove up, and Phil let go his second delivery. He put it around the knees, on the outside, and Prescott missed by a foot with a wild swing that sent him spinning.

"It would have been a ball, Prescott," Phil yelled at him. "What's the matter, are you rattled?"

Eyes blazing, the slugger threw his bat to the ground and started for the mound. But Vic Marshall said in a low voice, "Get back to the plate, Lew. This is a ball club, not a roughhouse." That was enough to stop the big man; he knew that Marshall meant what he said.

"O.K., hayseed," Prescott grated, picking up the stick again. "Just put one in here that I can tag onto. Just one!"

Phil grinned. "Here it comes," he said. "Let's see if your bat is as big as your mouth."

He breezed the third one in at shoulder-level. It was a floater and the stitches hardly turned. The ball moved with tantalizing slowness, a hard one to judge.

Prescott waited it out and then let go with another powerful swing. There was a hollow *crack!* as he got a piece of it, but it wasn't good enough and the horse-hide arched high into the air.

The ball was too far to Phil's right and too short for Steve Arnold at second. It was Joe Haslip's ticket; the speedy short fielder would be able to scoop it up and make the toss to first for an easy out. Phil turned to watch as Prescott dropped the bat and pistoned his legs down the chalk line.

Haslip went through the motions, but Phil saw immediately that the stocky blond was not working with his usual precision. It appeared to be a perfect play, but the scoop-up was a fraction slow and though Haslip snapped his arm, the drive to Bernie Wilson on the sack carried no power.

Prescott was safe by a good foot and a half.

It went the same way during the rest of his time on the mound. Phil pitched a good session but received no support from the other eight men on the side. They were working against him, turning easy outs into safe hits without taking errors.

Vic Marshall yanked Phil and put Charley Double on the rubber, and there was an immediate change in the men. They talked it up and played baseball the way the fans knew them. They were truly the Bruins now, showing the kind of form that made them perennial pennant favorites.

Bernie Wilson went twenty yards over the base line to drag down a pop-up. Joe Haslip picked up one from around his shoelaces and smashed it to first with a speed that was amazing. And Cliff Davis climbed the center-field wall to get a long hit by Hal Adams that would have been good for at least two. This was the way the Bruins played baseball when they wanted to —which they didn't when Phil was on the mound.

"How do you like those onions, kid?" Vic Marshall

said as he watched the performance. "Keep your eyes on old Charley Double and you'll pick up some diamond savvy that'll stand you in good stead. You've got to be able to sling them in there like he does, and you've got to make the boys play for you the way he does. That's why he's a great pitcher and not just another guy with a strong arm and a sure eye."

Phil knew he would be able to learn a lot from the old pitcher. He was living rhythm on the mound, making the ball perform wonders. That was what made Charley Double the kingpin of them all.

But making the team play for him was something else. That wasn't something you could learn from books, and Phil did not think he would be able to do it. The Bruins had shown that they did not want him on their team at all. They were against him and would not keep time with him no matter what tune he tried to play.

That evening, after dinner in the Hastings House where Vic Marshall had arranged a room for him, Phil sat in the lobby and tried to think it out. His first day with the Bruins had been a wash-out, and he didn't know what could be done about it.

But he was not sure he wanted to do anything about it. Baseball was the biggest thing in his life and he loved it. But if he made good in the big time he would be throwing old Charley Double out of the game, and that he didn't like.

He sighed and took an evening newspaper from the rack. He scanned the front page without interest, then turned to the sports section—and almost jumped from his seat. For there, over a two-column box, was a streamer and story about him! It said:

BRUINS TO START FLEDGLING AGAINST OWLS!

Vic Marshall, playing manager of the Bruins, threw a bomb into the baseball world by announcing that in tomorrow's opener against the Owls the veteran Charley Double would remain on the bench. Marshall said that orders had been received from Bud Fraser, owner of the Bruins, to start a newcomer named Phil Johnson on the mound.

Phil could not believe what the words told him. The Owls were running just a game and a half behind the Bruins for second spot in the league, and each of these games would carry a lot of weight. The Owls had got off to a slow start in the beginning of the season but had picked up somewhere along the line. If they topped the Bruins in this series there would be no stopping them and the pennant honors would probably fall into their laps.

Phil tried to reason it out, but there was no answer. The orders had come from Fraser himself, so it couldn't mean that Marshall was putting him on the mound because he wanted to. But why was Fraser doing it? That was the puzzler. The club owner should have known that Phil wasn't ready, that he'd hardly had enough time even to learn the signals that Stu Bacon would flash from behind the plate.

The next day Phil changed in the lockers surrounded by a cone of silence. He was being given the treatment and in a big way. It seemed that the Bruins had decided that if they couldn't bluff him out, they would make a good job of giving him the quick freeze.

And then Vic Marshall got up and gave them the usual pep talk. Only it seemed more like a funeral dirge than a shot in the arm. He was somber and obviously pessimistic about their chances, and he made it short and to the point.

After he finished Joe Haslip piped up with, "Toss the hayseed out, Vic, and we'll take the Owls easy. Start Charley and the series will be yours on ice."

"Yeah," Bernie Wilson argued. "It's crazy to take a chance on a green kid."

"All right, button it up!" the fiery manager snapped. "When Bud Fraser gives orders, we take them. Every one of us. He says that Phil Johnson goes on the mound —so he goes on the mound, and that's all."

Phil felt like a heel, and the men didn't mind letting him know that they felt the same way about him. But Marshall had given it to them straight: no one could do anything about it.

They were still grumbling when they filed out and made the motions of going through a warm-up. The stands were jammed, and Phil had never before seen so many people at one time. They were a noisy crowd, talking loudly and shouting derision and praise at the players, and Phil hoped they wouldn't start on him.

He worked out along the third-base line with Beef Burnham until his arm was well oiled, and before game time Charley Double walked from the dugout and came over to him.

"I know you can do it, boy," he said, slapping Phil on the back. "Just make like you're back in Northport and everything will be all right. Don't let those guys get you rattled."

The old pitcher sounded sincere, but Phil noticed a trace of anxiety in his eyes. And there was something else. There was regret there, too—regret and, Phil thought, a hint of sorrow.

Phil had butterflies in his stomach and they were holding a mass meeting. He knew his nervousness was written all over him, and he appreciated the boost the veteran was trying to give him.

"I—I'll try, Charley," he stammered. "And thanks."

"Swell." Charley Double grinned. "Now get out there and show your stuff!"

Phil choked up as he walked toward the mound. The biggest little god of them all—the man he was supposed to do out of a job—was wishing him luck. The guy had a heart as big as a milk bottle.

Then he was on the hill and his doubts grew larger. Pitching against the Bruins in practice was one thing, but doing it against the Owls for keeps was another. And he had no quarrel with the Owls, either, which made it that much harder.

"See if you can get them someplace near my glove, hayseed," Stu Bacon's hoarse voice cut into his thoughts. "I don't want to chase stray balls for you."

Phil twisted the sphere nervously in his glove without answering, and suddenly it was time to play. Ric Hammett, Owl left fielder, stepped up to the plate and took a couple of practice slices.

Stu Bacon signaled for a low one, around the knees,

on the inside. As Phil twisted he gritted his teeth in determination, then hauled back and let fly.

It was good, but Hammett let it go by for a called strike.

"Just wanted to see your steam." The Owl leadoff man grinned. "Next time I'll knock the hide off it, kid."

Stu Bacon called for a repeat performance, and Phil touched the rubber with his toe. The ball went down the groove and broke to the outside.

But something went wrong. Hammett's bat was there to meet it. Phil's spirits hit bottom as he heard the impact, but then he breathed easier when the ball flobbed foul.

"The next one's the ticket, hayseed!" Hammett yelled. "Just keep feeding them in like that."

Phil wound up again, his jaw set. Stu Bacon called for another low one, and Phil was going to put it right in the stocky catcher's mitt.

Then the fireworks broke. The ball was suddenly gone in a puff of white, and Hammett was running down the chalk line. He picked up two sacks before a hurried peg by Cliff Davis to Vic Marshall put the skids under him.

This wasn't good, Phil thought and sighed nervously. The first Owl up, and he clouts it for a double. It seemed to him that he was pitching all right, but he was too tight. He had to relax and take it easy.

But things didn't get any better. Phil pitched to Gurnie Marlow the way Stu Bacon instructed, and Marlow smashed out a hard single, driving Hammett to third.

"There goes the ball game!" Bernie Wilson moaned from first. "Oh, my aching back!"

And Joe Haslip rasped, "Let's get the guy a tin cup!"

Phil shook his head to keep the tears from coming, and then there was more work to do. Walt Heum, the Owls' power-puncher, was next on the ticket. Phil knew that if Heum tagged one there would be a conference on the field and Charley Double would come to the mound, while the waiver in his contract would be exercised and he would be shipped back to Northport.

He tensed and waited for Stu Bacon's signal. Then he caught it: a floater, right down the alley.

But that wasn't right, and Phil frowned. Why would Bacon call for such a pitch to Heum? Phil knew that a floater would end up on the other side of the fence.

He shook his head at Bacon, and then the catcher was walking toward him, his lips twisted. "Listen, hayseed," he growled, "you pitch them the way I call them. Understand?"

"Sure," Phil said. "I must have got the signal wrong. You couldn't have called for a floater."

"But I did," Bacon said. "And that's what I want, see?" He turned and walked from the mound.

Now Phil's head was spinning for sure. And then it was suddenly clear. Bacon was calling the wrong pitches because he wanted him out of the game!

The thought cleared his head and made his blood boil. All right, if that was the way they wanted it, he would dish out some of his own.

He sized up the slugger at the plate and made his decision. Hard hitters like to get under them, smashing up to get more distance. Well, he would just feed them in high, and on the inside.

The first one was a straight ball of fire, but it was too high and the umpire called it a ball. A look of surprise mingled with anger flashed across Bacon's face as he reached too late from his crouch and let the ball fly into the cage. But Phil didn't care how angry the catcher got; he was pitching his own game.

Stu Bacon again called for the floater, but Phil uncorked a hard outshoot. Heum took a called strike. He let the next one go for a ball, and missed the follow-up by inches.

The count was two and two, and Heum was still dangerous. He had stepped back to get away from those close ones and was poising the bat higher. So even though Bacon called for a low one on the inside, Phil slammed in a drop to the outside.

The umpire waved Heum away, and Phil sighed in relief.

Next up was Slim Atkins, the Owls' catcher, and Bacon called for an inshoot. Phil made his own choice and gave him a high floater which Atkins tapped only hard enough to pop out to Vic Marshall. Then Clint Jones came up and Phil knocked him down with three sizzlers that bounced like jumping beans. The side was retired with a befuddled Hammett and Marlow still sitting on the bags with no place to go.

Vic Marshall gave Phil a grin as they trotted to the dugout. "You had me scared there for a minute, boy," he said. "Hope it doesn't happen again."

"It won't," Phil promised. "Not like that, anyway. I learned a lot that inning."

The Owls took to the field, nine eager men with a lot of baseball experience. Olie Benson was on the mound, with Slim Atkins backing up. They were a good team, and their presence during the opener showed how much the Owls wanted to take the edge in these three games.

Bernie Wilson headed the Bruin line-up, and he took the count swinging. Olie Benson tossed them in with precision, and Bernie missed by a yard. Then Hal Adams stepped into the rectangle and let two go for one before he lifted the bat from his shoulder. He connected on the next one, a slow hook, and it looked good; but Walt Heum left his feet out in center and pulled it down. Frank Moscowitz was third up, and the count went to two and three before he popped out to Gurnie Marlow at short.

Phil never knew how he held the Owls down as the innings went by. It was hard work but he felt that it was up to him, since the Bruins had fallen off in their fielding. He couldn't understand where they had lost their pep, but they missed them too easily. Unless, of course, they were pulling the same business Stu Bacon had tried. He couldn't be sure.

The score remained at a pair of bulls'-eyes until the bottom of the seventh, when Joe Haslip and Cliff Davis singled, and both were driven home by Bernie Wilson's big stick. And then Olie Benson got back into business and made Hal Adams and Frank Moscowitz dizzy with his speed.

Phil went out and got to work again. He was feeling pretty good now, seeing those two markers go up on the scoreboard. Not bad for a hayseed, even if he did say so himself.

But then the ball game started coming apart at the seams. Phil's arm was tiring from the fast ones he had been tossing and the Owls started to latch on. He walked Olie Benson, and Steve Arnold, whom Vic had put in on the keystone sack, muffed a drive by Hunk Morgan. He put Hammett and Marlow out at the plate, and then Walt Heum lashed out a hard one that drove Olie Benson and Hunk Morgan home.

Phil felt that he was being given the short end of a raw deal. Those two errors had lifted the game right out of his hip pocket. The thought made him angry, and he fanned Slim Atkins to wind up the Owls.

"What's the matter, fellow?" Vic Marshall asked in the dugout. "Arm getting tired?"

Phil was still angry and he didn't try to hide it. "I'll be O.K.," he said heatedly. "Just tell those other guys I can't do *all* the work."

"Listen to the kid blow," Lew Prescott said. "Maybe he thinks we're twiddling our thumbs out there."

"You haven't been playing the Bruin way, that's all I know," Phil said. "If Arnold and Moscowitz hadn't been asleep they would have been able to stop those drives."

"I guess they walked Olie Benson too," Stu Bacon put in. "Don't forget, hayseed, he crossed the plate first."

Vic Marshall broke it up. "The next man that opens

his mouth," he said slowly, "gets a hundred-buck fine shoved in it. Now get out there and bring in some runs."

Bernie Wilson was first up. He let one go by for a ball, then tipped the second just enough to send it flying back into the cage. He got wood solidly on the next one, and it was a long drive to right. He was fast and slid into second a moment before Jesse Peck got the ball from Clint Jones.

Lew Prescott selected a bat and the field spread out. But he pulled a fast one and bunted. Atkins raced for the rolling sphere and scooped it up in time to throw Bernie Wilson out at third.

Steve Arnold was next in the batting order, and the only time he took the bat off his shoulder was to swing at one that would have been a ball by inches.

Then Phil came up. He was in a bad spot and he knew it. His pitching arm was all right but he was no great shakes at slamming them out. This time, though, he clenched his teeth in determination.

"Well, if it isn't the boy with the strong arm," Olie Benson grinned from the hill. "Here's out number three."

"Take it easy with the kid," Atkins taunted from behind his mask. "He's still got topsoil behind his ears."

Olie let go with a drop and Phil waited it out. He could see that it wasn't going to be good.

The umpire called it right.

Phil watched nervously as Olie Benson flexed his arm and looked over his shoulder at Lew Prescott on first. Then the ball was flashing down the alley.

It was meant to be an outshoot, but Phil saw that it was going to break too late. He tried to hit the dirt to get away from it, but he was a moment too late. The ball caught him a terrific wallop on the shoulder and sent him spinning.

The shoulder throbbed painfully, but Phil grinned as he trotted to first and advanced Lew Prescott to second. He hadn't struck out, anyway.

"Nice racket," Hunk Morgan grunted at him on the sack. "If you can't hit 'em, you let 'em hit you. That's one way for a bum pitcher to keep from being yanked."

"I'll remember that," Phil smiled, "the next time you come to the plate."

Then he was watching Cliff Davis in the rectangle. Davis was a good hitter, and if he got enough wood on it maybe he could drive Prescott home and tie up the game.

But Olie Benson had different ideas, and he laced them in hot. Davis went down on four pitched balls and Phil walked dejectedly from the sack to the mound.

Vic Marshall came out to see him and asked, "How's that shoulder, fellow? Will it hold up O.K.?"

Phil nodded. "I'll go the distance, don't worry."

Then he settled down to business on the Owls. He got Neil Shiff at the plate, and then Clint Jones came up and was knocked down. Phil was giving the ball everything he had and they couldn't touch it.

Next up was Slim Atkins. Phil pitched him a ball, two strikes, and another ball. Atkins somehow got his bat on the next one and it really traveled. It went out in a high arc and dropped into the bleachers.

It was the ball game, because Phil knew that Olie Benson wouldn't let the Bruins get near it in their half.

He was right, and when he went back to the lockers he felt completely washed up. He had dropped his first game for the Bruins—maybe his only game. And it hurt, especially since things had looked so good.

As he lowered himself to the bench by his locker it all spilled over. He buried his face in his hands and let it come. He knew he was making a fool of himself in front of a bunch of hardened ball players, but he couldn't help it.

"Look at the hayseed," he heard Stu Bacon say. "Crying like a baby—and after throwing a game like that!"

Phil jumped up, his eyes flaming. "Leave me alone," he warned, "or I'll show you how to throw something else!"

"Listen to the farmer rant," Bacon gloated. "As if he could—"

That was as far as he got. Phil's fist exploded on his chin and sent him toppling back against the lockers. The burly catcher came up bleeding from the mouth. He threw himself at Phil, pumping both arms, and then the other Bruins pulled them apart.

"That'll cost you guys a hundred dollars each," Vic Marshall said. "Now get under the showers and cool off. Next time it'll be two hundred and suspension."

The following day Phil got to the lockers early. He knew that Vic Marshall was going to hand him his walking papers, and he wanted to get one more look at that uniform with its big blazing "B" before being called up on the carpet.

The Bruins started filing in while he was still sitting there, and when they saw him they went silent again. It was the same treatment all over again.

Well, let them do what they want, he thought. He was still on the squad, and he was going to stay until the front office gave him other orders. He angrily peeled off his clothes and got into his uniform.

Charley Double came in as he was buttoning his shirt. "No use rushing yourself, boy," he said. "Vic wouldn't use you two days running."

"I know," Phil snapped, "but I can at least get a free look at the game. That's one thing this suit will do for me."

Charley frowned, then smiled again. "What's eating you, pal?" he asked. "You don't sound yourself."

Phil fumbled with the buttons, then forced a weak grin. "I'm sorry, Charley," he said. "I guess I got out of bed on the wrong side this morning."

The other players came in one at a time, and when Stu Bacon showed up, Phil noticed with satisfaction that his chin was blue and swollen. That punch had done more good than he had thought.

Vic Marshall came over and said, "How's your arm today, boy? Stiff?"

Phil flexed the shoulder that Olie Benson had hit. "It's all right. Not even sore."

"You'd better have Doc Gleason take a look at it anyway," Vic suggested. "A heat treatment probably wouldn't hurt any."

Phil grunted as the manager walked away. Vic was handing out the old sugar and spice only because it was his last day. Anyone could see that.

Then Vic read off the starting line-up. It was the same as in the opener, with one exception: Charley Double was starting on the mound. It was what the boys wanted, and their eyes started shining.

"Watch our steam today," Cliff Davis exclaimed. "Them Owls are as good as licked already!"

"You said it, kid," Hal Adams echoed. "Let's get out there and start things rolling."

Phil sat in the dugout and watched them. The team was different out there. They put showmanship into the warm-up and sparkled with talent. Even the fans liked the difference and one of them yelled, "Now we've got a *real* pitcher in there! Come on, you Bruins —murder them!"

The Owls came up and Charley buckled down. Ric Hammett was first in the box, and Charley worked it to two and two before the slugger tagged one that by rights should have gone over Joe Haslip's head. But the short fielder went deep on his bicycle and dragged it down between thumb and forefinger.

The spectacular stop brought a round of cheers from the fans, and Phil was so excited he swallowed his chewing gum.

Gurnie Marlow was next on the card, but he didn't do any better. He sent a waist-high drive down the third-base line, and Frank Moscowitz made the stop and whisked the ball to Bernie Wilson for an easy out.

The Bruins were a talking, laughing mob when they

trotted into the dugout after the third Owl had been knocked out. "We've got 'em by the eyeteeth," Lew Prescott said. "Boy, did that Charley pitch 'em dizzy!"

"That's the way things happen when we get a real hurler in there," Stu Bacon said, with a distasteful side glance at Phil.

Charley Double came over to Phil, his eyes bright with excitement. "Well, son," he said, "how did it look from here?"

Phil grinned at the veteran. "You bowled them over, Charley. It was really something to watch."

Charley shrugged it off. "I got only one," he admitted. "Shiff. I let Heum go for a walk, and you fanned him easy yesterday."

"O.K., boys," Vic Marshall's heavy voice boomed. "Let's see if you can handle a bat as well as you wag your tongues. Get out on the deck and put some runs up on the board."

But Bob Casey, on the mound for the Owls, had different ideas. He walked Bernie Wilson and let Hal Adams get a single before he warmed up. Then Frank Moscowitz, Lew Prescott, and Stu Bacon went down in order.

The Owls got two men on in the fifth before a long one by Clint Jones sent Hunk Morgan home. Charley Double walked the next man and loaded the sacks.

Things looked bad, and in the dugout Phil was going wild with anxiety. "Come on, fellows," he yelled. "Get 'em!" Then he saw Jesse Peck leave the circle. "He's a sucker for low hooks," he called to Charley. "Keep them down—around the knees!"

Charley flexed his arm and let it go. But it wasn't a low one; it was a high floater, and Phil closed his eyes as he heard the smack of wood against ball.

There was dead silence for a few seconds, and then the stands went up in a roar that sounded like a thousand cannon going off. The Bruins had somehow turned the hit into a double play, forcing Gurnie Marlow out at the plate!

The squad had been a little more somber each time after returning from the field, and this time the horseplay was completely gone. They sat on the benches and sighed as if they had been working hard, and Vic Marshall had to tell them to go to the circle.

Phil wanted to ask Charley Double how his arm was holding out but thought better of it. Instead, he said lightly, "That was a close shave out there. I wouldn't have been able to handle it the way you did."

"It was just dumb luck," Charley said tiredly. "Just dumb luck." The smile had just about faded from his face.

With one away, Vic Marshall got a single and Charley Double was given a free walk. Then Joe Haslip sacrificed and moved them down one more. The Bruins were in good scoring position for the first time, and Cliff Davis selected a bat and stood in the rectangle.

"Lay it on!" Bernie Wilson cried hoarsely. "Into the stands!"

The pitch came in. It was a high hook and Davis missed. He let the next one go for a ball, followed by a pop-up that went foul.

Tension increased in the dugout. Big Hal Adams was chewing his fingernails; Frank Moscowitz wasn't even watching; and Bernie Wilson was staring open-mouthed, his eyes wide.

Phil had never seen the mighty Bruins like this, and he was puzzled. They had played the field like maniacs, but what had happened to their punching power? It seemed to have gone down the same drain into which their fielding had poured during the opener.

Then Bob Casey uncorked the next one, throwing in a long overhand sweep that put plenty of push behind the ball.

Cliff Davis swung. And missed. The umpire waved him away from the plate and moans came from the dugout. The Bruins dragged themselves wearily from the benches and filed out to the field.

In the top of the seventh the Owls picked up another run, and when Charley at last cleared the side there were still two men on. If luck hadn't been riding the shoulders of the Bruins their nocturnal opponents would have tallied at least one more run.

When the players came in again and slouched to the benches Phil looked at them objectively. He couldn't understand what had happened; they had lost their fight, they acted completely defeated. He shook his head and grunted, wondering what the picture would be from here on in.

Joe Haslip turned tired eyes toward him and said, "What's the matter, hayseed? Maybe you don't like the way we're playing, huh?"

"I just can't figure it out, that's all," Phil said.

"Maybe they're too good for us," Cliff Davis put in. "Maybe they're—"

"And maybe you're too yellow!" Phil stopped him. "Maybe the whole bunch of you are laying down on the job!"

Lew Prescott got to his feet and loomed big over Phil, a dangerous light in his eyes. "Hold your tongue, kid," he warned. "When we want advice from your corner we'll ask for it."

"Yeah," Phil said. "Yeah, sure. You'll ask for it. You guys are the Bruins and you're too good to learn anything. That's the reason the Owls are trimming you out there."

Prescott grabbed Phil by the front of his shirt and yanked him to his feet. He pulled back a big fist and was about to let it go when Vic Marshall yelled, "Sit down—both of you! And that's a two-hundred-buck fine, Johnson, for inciting a fight in the dugout!"

Phil shoved Prescott away, his face red. "Better make it another hundred," he said, "because I'm not finished." He swept his eyes around at the players and grunted in distaste.

"So you guys call yourselves the Bruins, do you?" he said. "You're a bunch of dead beats, that's what. The kids I played with back in Northport had ten times as much fight as the whole mob of you put together!"

"Then shut up and go back to the sticks," Hal Adams exploded. "Nobody wants you around here."

"That's what I'm going to do," Phil said. "But first I want to tell you monkeys what I think of you—all except Charley Double. You didn't want me on the squad and didn't make any bones about letting me know it. O.K., now I'm telling you, you're a bunch of third-rate has-beens and I wouldn't want to be on the same field with you."

Vic Marshall said with authority, "Get into the lockers, Johnson. And stay there. And you guys get out there and slam in some runs. Hop to it."

Phil closed the locker door behind him and leaned heavily against it. "Well, little man," he sighed, "you've had a busy day, and that's for sure."

He walked slowly to the bench in front of his locker and started unbuttoning his shirt. He knew that even if Vic Marshall had planned to let him stay on the team another day, to finish the series, everything was washed up now. He would get his release right after the game.

He had made a mistake in blowing his top, but he couldn't help it. It was something that had been coming ever since he had walked into the lockers for the first time. The Bruins had given him the business, and he had handed it right back again. But it hadn't been because he held a grudge. It was because he was a Bruin as much as any of them—down deep, where it counted. And it hurt to see them falling down on the job like that.

Suddenly, after he didn't know how long, there was a muffled shout from the stands. It was the loudest racket he had heard during his time with the team, but he thought it probably only sounded louder because he was right under the stands. A few minutes later there was another shout, and then another that seemed powerful enough to cave in the roof over the lockers.

He didn't know what was going on; he was so low in spirits that he didn't care. But he knew that the shouts couldn't have come because of the Bruins. They must have meant that the Owls were up again and making mincemeat out of Charley Double's pitching.

And then, abruptly, the locker-room door was flung open and Muggs Roberts, the bat boy, raced in with excitement written all over his freckled face. He shouted, "They did it, they did it! It's the ball game!"

"What are you so happy about?" Phil said glumly. "You sound as if you had money on the Owls."

"Lew Prescott knocked one over the center-field fence with the bases loaded," Muggs rushed on. "They're playing like mad out there!"

Phil jumped up and scowled. "Who are you trying to kid? Those guys don't have enough fight in them to—"

"And Charley put the Owls down three in a row!" Muggs exclaimed. "I tell you, everybody is going crazy!"

This, Phil had to see, orders or not. He grabbed his shirt from the locker and ran out after the fleet youngster.

Then he saw that it was true. The scoreboard told the story: 5 to 2, with the Bruins on top! And the men in the dugout were bubbling with enthusiasm.

"You did it, son, you did it!" Charley Double yelled and wrapped both arms around Phil's neck. "You got those boys so mad they can't be stopped!"

"Yeah," Bernie Wilson added. "But we only got mad at ourselves, kid. You called our hand and we knew we were bluffing."

"And you can forget about those fines too," Vic Marshall said. "Matter of fact, there will probably be a bonus in it for you."

"Hold on a minute!" Phil yelled above the din. "You —you mean that I'm going to stay on the team—that you're not kicking me off?"

"Whatever gave you a screwy idea like that?" Vic said. "First time I saw you pitch I knew you had the stuff. Sure, you're a little rough around the edges, but those things can be ironed out."

Phil felt it coming again and the water bags behind his eyes filled up and spilled over. But this time it was different. He was laughing at the same time.

Then there was a rough voice from the side, saying, "Look at the kid crying—like a baby that wants a bottle." It was Stu Bacon, and Phil choked it off and turned to face him.

But this time the stocky catcher was grinning. He had a hand out and said, "Put it there, kid. I was wrong and I admit it. And," he added in a low voice, "I'm sorry about that other business. I mean—"

"Forget it," Phil said and took his hand. "I'll put them where you want them after this—if I think you're right."

Charley Double was talking again. "All right, calm down," he said. "I've got something to say." He waited a minute, then went on:

"I didn't tell you fellows before because—well, I

didn't know how to say it. But Fraser put Phil on the mound yesterday because I asked him to. You see"— his voice broke and faltered—"I'm getting too old for baseball. I—I'm going to retire after this series."

There was a shock of silence, and the veteran hurler continued quietly:

"I've played too many years, too many games, and my arm is going. It gets all of us sooner or later. I'm going to retire before the fans realize that I've slipped, that the Bruins win only because you boys work like horses to hold me up."

It was a dramatic speech for the sun-blackened man with the big smile, and it did something to all of them.

Phil was the first to find his voice, and he said, "Look, Charley, the team needs you. You're the spark that keeps it running. You've got to stay."

The old-timer shook his head. "No, son," he said. "It's all over. But there's one thing I want before I go. I'd like to just sit the rest of the game out and watch from the dugout. I want you to go out there and pitch this last inning, if your arm is all right. Sort of as a send-off for me. O.K.?"

Phil looked at Vic Marshall, and the manager nodded.

"And use my glove, Phil," Charley added. "It's out on the mound."

The Bruins brought in two more runs during the inning, but there was no yelling from the dugout. Then the Owl relief pitcher, who had been put in for Bob Casey, somehow got the third out.

"Well, let's go, boys," Vic Marshall said. "Let's put on a good show for old Charley."

Then they were on their feet and walking out to the field. Phil had a lump in his throat as big as the milk bottle that was Charley Double's heart, but it felt good there.

As he reached the mound and stooped over to pick up Charley's worn glove, a fan in the stands with a fog-horn voice yelled, "Look, it's the hayseed again. Smear them sleeping Owls, you hayseed!"

And Phil smiled and threw the guy a wave. Somehow, he no longer minded that word. It was—well, a sort of compliment.

Song of the Speedway

IT HAD BEEN two months since the accident, and Lou Andrews felt the cold fingers of apprehension digging in his spine as he sat stiffly on the side of the hospital cot. Nimble hands were doing things with scissors at the back of his head, and there was warm, even breathing on his neck. The doctor was removing the bandages from his eyes.

"Relax, son," Pokey Madison's voice suggested hoarsely. "It'll be all right. The doc says so."

"Certainly," came the professionally bored voice from behind him. "There's nothing to worry about. Absolutely nothing."

Lou grunted. Nothing to worry about, was there? That was easy for them to say. They hadn't been in the crack-up, and it wasn't their eyes. And they hadn't lived in a world of darkness for two long months, seeing the same chilling scene unfolded over and over again in their mind's eye. That's the reason it was so easy for them. They didn't know what it was like to crash from the roaring road at a hundred miles an hour.

Then his thoughts froze. The cutting had stopped and there was a cool band around his head as the doctor unwound the bandages. In a few seconds they were off and heaped beside him on the cot. But Lou did not try to open his eyes.

"It's all right now, Mr. Andrews," the doctor said with assurance. "Don't be afraid."

With the icy fingers clawing tighter at his spine, Lou forced his eyelids apart. Then he snapped them together again. The lights in the room had been dimmed and the blinds drawn, but still it was too much for his sensitive pupils.

"Come now, Mr. Andrews," the doctor said softly. "You have to expect some light blindness. After all, it has been—"

"Yeah," Lou broke in, suddenly opening his eyes. "It's been two months. That's a long time to be dead, a whale of a long time!"

His anger abruptly cooled and he regretted his outburst. The light still seemed bright, but he could see. His eyes were all right.

"There, I told you," the doctor said, unperturbed. "As good as new. You'll be able to go home after we make a few simple examinations." He left the room, to get his test equipment.

Pokey Madison, Lou saw, was wearing a relieved smile on his florid face. Short, and heavy to fatness, he had added a few new gray streaks to his thinning hair these past months.

"How do you feel, son?" he asked. "Eyes O.K.?"

"Sure, Pokey," Lou said warmly. "They're all right. Everything is kind of bright, but I guess it'll pass."

Pokey clapped his hands together. "Good! We'll give them a few more days, and then you'll want to get over to the track. I guess your hands are itching to get on a wheel again."

Lou shook his head. "I told you," he insisted, "I'm through with the racing game. I don't care if I never see another mill."

Pokey's smile turned to a frown. "But *Miss Shammy's* all rebuilt, son. She's as good as new, without even a dent in her hood. I've been working on her ever since it happened."

Lou was still shaking his head. "I'm sorry, Pokey, but the closest I'll go to a racer from now on is the bleachers."

"Then what am I going to do?" Pokey argued. "I can't drive her myself!"

"Get yourself another boy, or sell her." Lou was definite.

The little owner's eyes clouded in disappointment. He'd had such great plans laid out for the two of them, and now it seemed that they were washed down the drain.

"You're making a mistake, boy," he said slowly. "You think you can just snap your fingers and say you're not going to race any more, but it's not that easy. You've got castor oil in your blood and track dirt in your pores, and you can't get rid of them. You've heard the song of the speedway, and you'll never forget the tune."

Lou shook his head still again. "I've made up my mind, and that's the way it is."

Pokey said, "Then what are you going to do?"

Lou shrugged. "I don't know. Maybe knock around for a month or so and take things easy."

"And then what? You'll still have to eat."

Lou had an answer ready. He had figured it out while

lying on the hospital cot. He knew cars and engines better than anything else, and had decided to open a garage.

But when he told Pokey Madison of his plans the little owner just grunted. "It'll cost a lot to open a garage," he said. "What will you use for money?"

Lou didn't understand what he was talking about. "My bank account, of course," he said. "I haven't just blown away all the purse money I've collected."

"What about the hospital bills? You've been here two months. You've had a private room and private nurses. You've had specialists taking care of your eyes. How much money do you think you'll have left when you finish handing it over to them?"

Lou had not even thought of the hospital expenses, and the sudden realization that these expenses existed came to him as a shock. But he soon recovered and said, "Don't worry about me, I'll be all right."

"Well, I certainly hope so," Pokey said. "But do me one favor, son. Just for old-time's sake. Come around and take a look at *Miss Shammy* after you're feeling better. I won't even ask you to try her out; I just want you to see how her face has been lifted. O.K.?"

Lou said that he would, and Pokey went on, "Then we won't talk about it any more. I'll go outside now and wait, while the doc looks you over. Good luck, boy."

A few seconds later the doctor came in with his instruments, and as he went through his prerelease checkup Lou had another mental picture of that day two months before.

It was the forty-second lap of a scheduled fifty-circuit dirt-track grind at the Hammersmith Speedway. He had been battling with Slick Valle and his silver chariot since the opening flag, with the honor slot see-sawing back and forth between them. But now Lou was giving *Miss Shammy* everything she was worth, with the power pin clamped hard on the floor boards, and the little mount was kicking and bucking with the dizzy speed.

But Slick Valle would not be passed. His silver racer wasn't as fast as the crimson *Miss Shammy,* but the veteran driver had plenty of track knowledge and knew how to keep a faster job from heeling his rear shoes.

Slick started easing over as they came out of the west turn and hit the stretch in front of the stands. He forced Lou over to the inside rail, holding him tight without enough room to get out. Then suddenly he was away.

And Lou had let out a hoarse scream. He saw why Valle had pulled over, but not soon enough. An excited young boy of not more than ten or twelve had run out onto the track—and he was right in Lou's path, either blind or senseless to the danger!

Lou had tried with all his might to brake *Miss Shammy,* but the speed was too great, and there wasn't enough time to skid to the outside. There was only one thing he could do to keep from killing the boy. He closed his eyes and twisted the wheel savagely to the inside, cutting the switch as he rammed into the flimsy wooden rail.

Lou clamped his eyes shut to block out the scene, and the doctor said, "Mr. Andrews, if you please. This is a delicate test, and I must have your co-operation."

True to his promise, Pokey Madison did not say another word about racing. But Lou could tell from little things around the apartment they shared that he had not forgotten. Like the time he left the newspaper open to the page announcing the Springvale hundred-lap classic, with a purse of $6,000—leaving it where Lou couldn't possibly miss it. And then, after the fifth day, Pokey started looking at him questioningly and Lou knew he would have to make that visit to the track.

But when he saw the sparkling new *Miss Shammy* he was not sorry he had made the decision. He hadn't seen the little racer since Hammersmith, but from all he had heard he was lucky to be alive. *Miss Shammy,* from all accounts, had been little more than a twisted mass of smoldering scrap iron good only for the junk heap; but somehow the magic of Pokey Madison's stubby fingers had brought back and even improved her former trim lines.

"Beautiful, isn't she?" Pokey said with pride. "And you ought to see her step, Lou. There's not another mill this side of Indianapolis that can keep up with her."

"You did a swell job," Lou admitted, running his eyes over the smooth lines appraisingly. "Must have been tough work."

"Wasn't anything, son," Pokey said seriously. "It was all for you. Want to—want to give her a spin?" he added anxiously.

Lou debated with himself for a moment. Two months ago he would have given an arm and a leg to sit behind the wheel of a car like this, but now it was different. There was a slight itch in his hands, but not enough for him to break his resolve. He was finished with racing, and nothing could get him back to it again.

"Thanks," he answered, "but no thanks. I knew you were figuring I'd change my mind if I saw *Miss Shammy,* but it's no good, Pokey. I'm finished."

Pokey sighed deeply. "Well, you can't blame me for trying. Are you still going to open that garage?"

Lou nodded. "I haven't changed my plans."

The little owner grinned. "I guess that means you haven't seen the bill from the hospital."

"That's right," Lou admitted. "They haven't said anything about charges, and I can't understand it."

Pokey's grin widened. "It's probably because they've got too many things to add up. No, sir, I don't think I would make any plans for opening a garage just yet, if I were you."

"Well, I'll go ahead with them anyway," Lou said angrily. "I told you I was through with racing, and I meant it."

"It was just an accident that that boy got out on the track," Pokey insisted. "Those things don't happen but once in a lifetime."

"And that's once too often," Lou snapped. "It took something out of me. I—I'm afraid to drive. I'm afraid I'll crack up again."

"You know what airplane pilots say," the little owner went on. "When they have a smash they get in another plane and take off right away. That's so it won't get under their skin."

"But it's already under my skin," Lou said, and turned away from *Miss Shammy*. "I'll see you around, Pokey, but not at the races. I'm moving out and getting a room of my own."

Lou thought that would fix everything, but it didn't. He got a room in a hotel and tried to forget about racing and everything that went with it. But he found himself automatically turning to the sports pages and looking for news of the Springvale. He tried to tell himself that it was just passive interest, but deep down he knew it wasn't so.

Pokey had been right that day at the hospital, and Lou knew it. He had castor oil in his blood and race track dirt in his pores, but he was still afraid. He had come face to face with the grinning image of Death at Hammersmith, and his nerve was gone. He trembled every time he thought about skidding around a turn or pumping a throttle. The spark had flickered and gone out, he told himself, and nothing could bring it back again.

He was worried, too, about the hospital bill. He couldn't understand why it was delayed, and he couldn't follow through on his plans with the garage until he had some indication of the final amount of money he would have left from his savings.

Then the Springvale was only two days away, and Pokey Madison came to see him. Pokey looked worried, and his eyes were bloodshot, his face drawn and pale.

"Look, son," he said quietly. "I'm going to lay it on

the line, and for the last time. I haven't been able to find a driver worth his salt to wheel *Miss Shammy*, and I still want you in the bucket seat. What do you say?"

Lou shook his head. "I'd like to help you out, Pokey, but the answer is still the same. I just can't do it."

"Suppose I offered you a thousand dollars? Just this one race. Then you could open that garage for sure."

Lou was tempted, but then that accident scene flashed before him again and he knew he wouldn't be able to do it.

"I won't even ask you for first place," Pokey persisted. "Just in the top three."

Lou frowned. "Are you feeling all right, Pokey? If I took third and you gave me a thousand dollars, you wouldn't even make expenses. That doesn't sound like good business to me."

"I don't care about that, son," the little owner said. "I think I've got something bigger to play for. Remember I said I did some work on *Miss Shammy*'s engine? Well, I hit on an idea in carburetion that should interest the big motor men in Detroit. All I've got to do is prove it in an actual race."

Lou was immediately interested, and he listened intently as Pokey Madison explained how he had changed the carburetor jets by accident, and how it had given him greater power and almost double the mileage. It was something that the best scientists had been trying to do for years.

But though the thought intrigued him, Lou still could not shake off the fear hammering at the back of his head, and he said, "I'll put *Miss Shammy* through any kind of tests, Pokey. But I won't go out on the track in competition. I wouldn't be able to do it, and you'd just be throwing away your thousand dollars."

"Then I'll tell you what," Pokey quickly suggested. "You just come out and run her around a few times. I haven't told anybody else about this carburetor business, and I'd like to know what you think. I've got my car downstairs, and we can get to Springvale in a couple of hours. What do you say?"

Lou couldn't very well say no to a request like that, and late that afternoon they were at the Springvale Speedway, in the pits with *Miss Shammy's* cowl unbuckled.

". . . That's the way it works," Pokey was explaining. "The reason nobody thought of it before is because it's too simple."

Lou scratched his head in puzzlement. "What's the difference whether you introduce air into the intake before the gas gets to the carburetor? I don't get it."

"But it works," Pokey insisted. "Take her around a few times and you'll see how much pep she's got."

Just then Slick Valle appeared from somewhere and said, "Well, well, if it isn't Lou Andrews in person. What are *you* doing around Springvale? I heard you had turned yellow."

Lou turned slowly and looked at Valle. He had never thought much about it before, but now suddenly he didn't like the driver. He didn't like his superior manner of speaking, he didn't like that trick waxed mustache, and he didn't like the spotless silver coveralls emblazoned with the fancy S. V.

He said between clenched teeth, "Go fry, Valle."

"And miss the chance of winning the Springvale?" the veteran driver returned. "That purse money is as good as in my bank account right now. There won't be any competition at all—not a thing for me to worry about."

"That's only because Lou's not going to be in there," Pokey put in heatedly. "You wouldn't stand a chance against *Miss Shammy* with Lou at her wheel."

Valle said unpleasantly, "Stop blowing off steam, you old fool. I could lick—"

That was as far as he got. Lou didn't care what anyone called him, but they weren't going to talk to Pokey like that while he was around. All of his suppressed anger surged to the surface, and he threw a fast right hook to Valle's chin and sent him staggering back on his heels.

Valle got up with his eyes blazing. But then he smiled and brushed his coveralls carefully.

"No use fighting that way, Andrews," he said evenly. "But I challenge you to meet me Saturday afternoon at the starting line. Let's see if you've got enough guts to show up, or if you're the yellow quitter everybody says."

"O.K., Valle, you're on," Lou said quickly without thinking. "And stay away from me, or I'll show you what it's like to go through the rail!"

Valle walked away stiffly, and Pokey said, "You didn't mean that, boy. He'll spread the word around that you're going to race, and when you don't show up for the flag the newspapers will build a fire under you.

That won't do your garage any good, and it won't help me either."

"I'll be there all right," Lou said angrily. "If Valle is too much of a coward to fight with his fists, I'll fight him the way he wants."

Incredulity showed on Pokey Madison's face. He began, "But you said—"

"Forget what I said," Lou interrupted. "I'll take that offer of yours, but you can keep your thousand if they don't give me the checkered flag."

Miss Shammy made the qualifying run the next day with ease, and Lou and Pokey made last-minute adjustments on the gleaming racer.

"Well, what do you think now that you've wheeled her around?" the little owner asked with a grin. "Sweet, isn't she?"

"The race is in the bag," Lou promised. "I never thought I'd want to come back to the track, but this little mill has convinced me. We'll take that Slick Valle like the Yanks took Germany."

And then it was Saturday afternoon and time for the classic. The huge grandstand on the north side of the two-mile brick track started filling early, and half an hour before flag time it seemed impossible that any more fans could be squeezed in. But still they came— excited speed-mad maniacs buying thrills and spills at two dollars a throw.

In the pits, Pokey Madison looked at Lou with anxious eyes. "Are you sure you're going to be all right, boy?" he asked. "I mean, if you're still afraid of the track—even a little—I don't want you to go out there."

"I'm shaking right down to my toes," Lou admitted. "But I'm trying to tell myself that the other crack-up happened only this morning and that it hasn't got under my skin yet. I'm trying to be like those pilots you told me about."

"You mean you're scared and you're still going to go through with it?"

Lou bobbed his helmeted head. "I'm not going to give the newspapers a chance to roast me. I'm going out there and beat the wind out of Slick Valle or blow up this boiler trying."

Pokey slapped him warmly across the back. "O.K., boy," he said. "It's time to get out on the line and show your stuff. I won't wave you in unless it's important."

Miss Shammy drew the third row, second outside position. She was flanked by Al Travers in an Allison-powered mount and Joe Binley in an all-white Fiat. Slick Valle's silver special was in the first row, Number Two slot. His showing at the Hammersmith Speedway and low time during the qualifying runs had earned him the prized position.

Lou's throat was constricted with tension and his hands were claws on the corded wheel. He had never felt like this before a race, but he had never been in a crack-up before either. He felt like screaming, or jumping out of the gleaming racer, or roaring away at full throttle—anything to break the strain of just sitting there and waiting.

Suddenly the pace car out in front started moving, and the Springvale grind was under way. Lou yanked the goggles down over his eyes and cleared *Miss Sham-*

my's throat with a heavy foot. He still felt the urge to jump from the cockpit and run, but now it was too late. He was committed to race and take Slick Valle's challenge.

They marched once around the oval in parade formation, two dozen roaring juggernauts straining at the leash. And then the pace car disappeared and the starter's flag whisked down, transforming the mild afternoon into a screaming inferno as heavy feet clamped hard on power pins.

Lou's tenseness was abruptly gone with the excitement of the race, and he was forced to give the wheel his full attention. Joe Binley's Fiat started to skid on the smooth bricks with the quick surge of power, and Lou had to ease away without sideswiping Al Travers. It was a tight spot for a split second, but then Binley got his car under control.

Lou was still far to the outside when they went into the banked west turn, and he started easing in toward the pole, taking his chances when he could. A sky-blue twin-overhead job faltered slightly as they bulleted out of the turn, and Lou shot into the gap, putting *Miss Shammy* one lane closer to the short inside position.

Time became static as the laps flew by. At the thirty-fifth circuit the field was still jumbled, though thinning a bit as the slow jobs fell behind and the faster ones moved up, and *Miss Shammy* was no better than eleventh in line. Slick Valle was nowhere in sight, but as Lou flashed past the stands he heard the squeaking voice of the public address system saying that the silver racer was out in front.

Lou grinned. Maybe Valle had the slot honors now, but wait till he gave *Miss Shammy* her head. Then he would show the guy with the trick mustache that he could fight with a racer as well as with his fists.

The thought of the duel to come made him squash down a bit more with his right foot. *Miss Shammy's* churning power plant started pounding faster in a deep, throaty scream of defiance as she took the gas and surged forward. Lou went into the west turn with his foot still heavy, pumping the brake to keep from skidding, and yammered past two boys hugging the pole.

He came out into the stretch with a burst of speed and singing tires, then eased up. There was still plenty of time to make his bid, and he wasn't in any hurry. All he wanted right now was to pull up a little at a time.

At the sixty-second lap he had worked up to fifth, and he knew that from here on it would be smooth running. He was back in the groove again and had forgotten about that business in Hammersmith.

Then Bill Hunt's Spartan, up in the heel position behind Slick Valle, suddenly started having trouble. Hunt wasn't aware of it yet, but Lou's startled eyes saw the axle beginning to push through the Spartan's left rear hub!

"Pull over!" Lou screamed. "You're going to crash, Hunt! You're—"

And then it happened at blinding speed. The rear of Hunt's car collapsed and dragged along the bricks in a shower of sparks and smoke. Hunt tried to fight it, to keep his control. But it was no good. The Spartan slued wildly for a moment, and then bucked over to the outside and scrouged against the cement guard wall.

The projector in Lou's brain switched on again and he went numb all over. Hunt had come out of the mishap without serious injury, but only by the sheerest scrape of good fortune. If one of his wheels had flown off, or if it had been a wooden railing, Hunt wouldn't have had a chance. Lou lifted his foot from the throttle as if it were a booby trap, and after the turn he pulled into the pits.

Pokey Madison came running over as the crimson racer braked to a stop, a frown on his face.

"What's wrong, boy?" he asked anxiously. "Gas?"

Lou shook his head. "I can't do it, Pokey," he said. "I can't. I thought it was going to be all right, but then—"

"You mean Hunt's spill?" Pokey broke in. "But he wasn't hurt. He walked away from it!"

"Only by luck," Lou said slowly. "The next time it might be me, and I wouldn't have the same kind of luck."

"Look," Pokey said seriously. "Some people get killed just walking across the street, some fall downstairs and break their neck, and I've even read about people slipping in the bathtub and killing themselves. You've had one smash, and chances are you'll never have another."

Lou shook his head. "I can't take that chance, Pokey. I—I'm scared."

The little owner's face went pale, and he picked up

the gas hose and started siphoning fuel into *Miss Shammy's* tank. Then, hurriedly replacing the cap, he said, "Get out of the pit. I'm finishing the race myself."

"What!" Lou exclaimed. "But you haven't driven a racer in years!"

Pokey grabbed a helmet and pulled it over his balding head. "Maybe I haven't—but I'm not yellow. Now, get out of my mill."

Lou's jaw suddenly hardened. He knew that Pokey would get himself killed if he tried to wheel *Miss Shammy* around those banked turns, and the determined gleam in the little owner's eyes told him that he was set on trying.

"Are you going to get out," Pokey said in a low voice, "or do I have to drag you out?"

Lou snapped the goggles down over his smeared face. "You're not driving today," he said. "If the race means that much to you, I'll take the checkered flag or wrap up trying."

Miss Shammy coughed once from the surge of raw gasoline and then catapulted out onto the speedway. Lou's face was set in a grim mask, and he went into the turn without using his brakes, coming out into the backstretch with the throttle still split wide open.

The way he felt now, he didn't care what happened to him. Pokey Madison had been ready to throw his life away for the carburetor under *Miss Shammy's* hood. Well, Lou thought, if that's the way he wants it, I'll give it to him!

He threw the yammering mill around like a scooter

bike. On the long straightaways he pushed his foot hard to the fire wall, and on the turns he slewed and skidded until the churning rear shoes threatened to rip themselves off.

But he picked up his lost time, and as they came out of the east turn at the end of the eighty-first lap he was thundering along behind Joe Binley's all-white Fiat in third place.

Binley heard Lou coming up, and he shot a quick glance back over his shoulder and tried to squeeze more power out of his imported engine. But it wasn't good enough to match *Miss Shammy*'s ultrahigh compression, and Lou shot past him on the outside.

Now Slick Valle was the only one in front of him, and Lou grunted. The silver racer was fast and the man at the wheel was good, but they weren't enough to worry *Miss Shammy*. She had shown herself capable of taking the silver special's measure more than two months ago, and that was before Pokey Madison had jazzed up her engine.

Lou took it easy for a few laps, coming up slowly, and when they came around for the eighty-ninth he made his bid. His foot squashed hard on the power pin and the red racer's wheels screamed in protest. The surge of power pushed him back in his seat, and his white-knuckled fingers clamped harder on the bouncing wheel.

He came up in the heel position on the outside of Slick Valle, and then had to ease out at the turn. When they hit the backstretch he pulled up again, but this time Valle was riding the middle of the track. Lou grinned and quickly wheeled into the pole slot, thinking that Valle had made a mistake.

But the silver-clad driver had been waiting for just that move. As Lou pulled his front wheels into the gap, Valle lurched closer, wedging him in. Not enough to make him crash, but close enough to keep him from going through.

They stayed like that down the backstretch, Lou waiting for a break and Valle not giving any. Then he had to ease back to keep from skidding on the turn.

They went through the same routine for five laps, and Lou's nerves wore ragged. The crack-up picture started to flash through his mind again as they sped into the backstretch, and his foot lifted from the throttle for a split second. Then he shook his head and lead-footed it once more.

"All right, mister!" he yelled into the slip stream. "I'm coming through!"

Valle held him against the pole, but Lou kept his eyes straight ahead and bored in. Once, his left front tire just barely scraped the wall and there was the squeal of burning rubber. The wheel jerked in his hand, but it was not enough to throw him out of control.

Slowly he squeezed through the hole, with Valle not giving an inch. Their racing wheels were even when they came to the turn, and neither of them hit the brake.

Sweat came out on Lou's face and his heart started

to pound. This was the payoff, and he knew that if he skidded the cars would lock together and crash off the speedway.

He toyed the wheel gingerly, trying to keep the rear wheels steady. Then, as the turn sharpened, he felt *Miss Shammy*'s rear start to go light. He fought to keep the bouncing mill steady, but his foot remained hard on the throttle.

He shot a quick look at Valle. The silver-clad driver's face was impassive as he fought his mount. But he was going away slightly. The special was lighter than the underslung *Miss Shammy* and couldn't hug the track as well.

Then Lou's wheels went into a slight skid, but there was enough room and they didn't come even close to Valle. The danger was past, and Slick Valle smiled strangely and threw a quick salute as he fell behind.

Lou sighed in relief as he came out into the straightaway. Valle had fought and lost, and now there was nothing ahead except clear road.

Four laps later he got the white flag, and then once more around with nothing to worry about and he was waved in with the checkered. Lou exhaled sharply as he rolled into the pits and Pokey Madison came running over.

The little manager was jumping up and down and shouting crazily. "You did it, boy!" he yelled. "First place in the Springvale!"

Lou smiled tiredly and lifted the goggles from his burning eyes. "Now you can cash in on that carburetor, Pokey," he said. "I guess it proved itself, all right."

"Carburetor?" Pokey said, grinning. "That was just a gag, son, so I could get you out to the track."

Lou's eyes widened. "You mean—"

"I mean I didn't want you to throw your life away in a garage," Pokey cut in. "You're a race-car driver, and nothing else. You'll never be able to sing anything except the song of the speedway, but I had to make you remember the tune."

Lou frowned, and then his face cracked in a smile. "I guess it's just as well," he said. "The garage was only a dream anyway. Those hospital bills would have taken all my money."

Pokey shook his head. "You would have had plenty of money. You see, there wasn't any hospital bill at all. After your crash at Hammersmith, the drivers all pitched in for your expenses. They figured you deserved it, for going through the rail to save that boy.

"And don't feel sore at Slick Valle either," Pokey raced on. "That was some sock you gave him, but he was part of the act too. He figured that if he could make you mad enough you would drive against him just to get even. We had it all figured out, boy. You couldn't win!"

Lou wiped a hand across his puzzled eyes. Pokey had pulled three fast ones on him, but now that it was over he was glad. He was mixed up and happy, but he was no longer afraid. And suddenly he had a crazy urge to start singing the only song he would ever know —the screaming, pounding song of the speedway.

A Pitch in Time

EMMETT MASON sat hunched over on the bench, toying a baseball between his lean fingers and looking absently at the stitches while Chuck Brislow, the Eagles' grizzled manager, wound up his pregame instructions.

He was big and red haired, this Emmett Mason, with the kind of a face you would never look at twice in a crowd. But he had a brain on his beefy shoulders and could never learn too much about the weaknesses of the men he was to pitch against.

Ordinarily, that is. Right now he was not listening; he had something more important on his mind.

He flexed his shoulder and grimaced. The twinge was still there, as he had expected. He had baked the shoulder all that morning and used liniment until the skin was tender. But still there was no improvement. The hurt was down deep, in the bone, where the heat and liniment had not reached.

But how could he tell Chuck Brislow that he was in no condition to pitch? They would be counting on his fast ones today, and besides, such things couldn't be explained. Chuck had once accused him of having a pound of butter for a heart, and if Emmett told him how he had ruined his arm, and for what purpose, there would probably be other words, some of them not too complimentary.

There was a sudden silence in the locker room. Something that Emmett sensed rather than heard. He raised his eyes to Chuck, and Chuck was looking at him strangely.

"Well," the manager said patiently, "what do you think?"

Emmett realized that Chuck had asked him a question, and he didn't know what to say.

"Hope I didn't disturb you. I was just wondering if you thought you could hold the Tigers today."

"Sure," Emmett said. "Sure I can. Why—"

"O.K., boys," Chuck went on. "Hop out there and warm up. Get the joints good and greased, because it's going to be a tough one." He added, "You wait, Emmett."

The squad started talking it up as they filed from the lockers, their shoes scraping and clomping on the cement floor. But Emmett just sat there, still hunched over. He knew what Chuck Brislow wanted to talk about and he couldn't make up his mind how to answer.

When the room was empty the Eagles' manager came over and dropped to the bench next to him. He said quietly, "What's eating you, fellow? You've got something on your mind."

"It's nothing," Emmett said, trying to sound convincing. "I'm all right."

"I've never seen you like this before. You didn't hear anything I said about the Tigers."

"I know how to pitch to them," Emmett said. "You don't have to worry about that."

Chuck studied him closely for a few seconds, his

gray eyes searching. "You don't want to talk about it?"

Emmett shook his head. "There's nothing to talk about."

Chuck put his hands on his knees and pushed to his feet, grunting. "If you decide that there is something to talk about, I'll be ready to listen. In the meantime, you'd better loosen up that arm."

As Emmett walked out to the field he thought about that business last night and wondered how he could have done anything so crazy. He had been in the lobby of the hotel, wondering what to do, when the girl had come over and started talking to him. Her name was Alice Rivers, she told him, and she said that she was an Eagle fan, and particularly an Emmett Mason fan.

He thought she was the most beautiful girl he had ever seen, with honey-colored hair and laughing eyes as blue as the middle of the ocean. After a few minutes they had become very friendly and Emmett was using her first name as if he had known her for years. Yet there was something about the situation that bothered him. What kind of girl would speak to a guy unintroduced—even though she might be a fan?

A half an hour later they were at the carnival on the outskirts of town. Alice lived in the neighborhood, and she had suggested it for laughs.

They rode the Ferris wheel and the caterpillar and the whip, and then they started making the rounds of the stalls. They stopped at one booth, watching the customers trying to knock wooden milk bottles from a platform with pitched balls, and Alice had seemed intrigued.

"I've always wanted a kewpie doll," she had said. "Win one for me, Emmett."

Even then he had realized that it wasn't the smartest thing to do, but he couldn't resist the temptation to show off just a little.

The first six balls had been wasted, warming up his arm and getting the range. And then he settled down and threw with precision. But the balls were light and had to be thrown hard to scatter the loaded milk bottles, and by the time Alice had her kewpie doll Emmett's arm had a peculiar feeling.

Still the girl was not satisfied. She wanted another doll—for her young sister, she said. When Emmett finished pitching the second time his shoulder was twitching, and in the morning it was stiff and sore. . . .

The stands filled early and at game time they had become a sea of howling faces. Emmett knew that the Eagle fans up there were counting on him to hold the Tigers down, but he didn't see how he would be able to do it. The workout had not helped his shoulder; it still pained with every movement and he knew that he would not be able to throw his fast one.

"This is it, boys," Chuck Brislow said in the dugout. "We have to come out on top in this series to stay in the race. Give those guys everything you've got, and then pile on a little more."

He walked with Emmett toward the mound, and said, "This is your last chance to talk about it before things get rolling. Might be good to get it off your chest."

"I'm O.K.," Emmett said again. "There's nothing to talk about."

Chuck looked at him quizzically. "You're sure?"

"I'm sure. Those Tigers don't worry me."

Chuck cuffed him across the back, and he almost collapsed from the pain. "Here's luck, then. Get them fast and don't take any chances."

Emmett continued on out to the hill, his shoulder a throb of torment. It had been bad enough before, but the ache was so bad now he didn't see how he would even be able to go into a windup.

He tossed a few to Hank Winters, the blond backstop, and then the first Tiger came up to the plate. It was Ben Kantor, an outfielder, and the lanky southpaw with steel in his wrists liked it shoulder-high on the inside. He was batting two fifty-three for the season and was always a threat.

Hank called for a low one, on the outside, and Emmett wound up slowly. His shoulder grated with each twist but he had to make it look well for the fans. He was afraid to put too much behind it, and even as the ball left his fingers he knew that it wasn't going to be good.

It was well on the inside, below the knees, and Kantor stepped back. Hank had been expecting a steamer, but there was only a hollow sound when the ball plopped into his mitt. He frowned through his mask before tossing it back again.

The Tiger coaches at first and third opened up with a barrage of torments, and loud catcalls came from the dugout. A called ball on the very first heave was something they hadn't expected, and they were making the most of it. Ordinarily, Emmett would have answered them with a grin, but today he didn't feel in the mood.

"Knock him down, kiddo," Al Brown called from the keystone sack. "Feed the guy your fast one and then let's hear them laugh!"

Hank Winters signaled for another low one and Emmett tried to put it in. He concentrated, this time, but still he held back. Too much steam, he thought, and his arm would follow the ball down the groove.

It floated in with too much space under it, and Kantor swung. It was a solid hit, landing just short of the left field bleachers, and the southpaw beat it to second in a slide.

The Tigers went wild. They knew from experience that Emmett Mason was a tough hurler to hit and they had never expected the leadoff man to get wood on it. Their taunts and catcalls were doubled, and the sea of fans added their own voices to the turmoil.

Emmett picked up the resin bag with nervous fingers. He wasn't worried about the first Tiger up getting a hit. But he was worried about all the others yet to step into the rectangle, and the condition of his arm.

Hank Winters walked out from behind the plate, concern written on his face. "You all right, Emmett?" he asked. "The ball doesn't seem to have much push."

Emmett wiped his hands with the resin bag. "Just feeling them out," he said. "Don't worry about this end."

"Then let's get some hot ones in there. Knock them down, boy."

Steve Luke was next up. An old-timer who knew every trick there was to know, he was a methodical hitter who could place them with pinpoint precision. He liked to crowd the plate, elbows waving, and was apt to take a cut at anything that came down the alley.

Emmett took the glove from his hip pocket and Hank Winters signaled for a high one on the inside, to force Luke back from the plate. He looked over his shoulder at Ben Kantor dancing off second, and toed the rubber. He flexed his arm and threw, and the twinge was still there, tugging at his muscles.

Luke let it go by for a called strike. "Give us a good fast one, sonny boy," he taunted. "I'll put it over the fence for you!"

He took the ball again and looked toward the dugout. Chuck Brislow was standing up, watching him anxiously. This wasn't the Emmett Mason the team's manager had known for the past three seasons—not the powerhouse rubber man who could make the ball hop around like a jumping bean. It was somebody Chuck hadn't seen before, and he didn't like the way it looked.

"Come on, kid, toss him silly," Bill Lopez urged from first. "Let's get moving."

"That guy move?" taunted the Tiger coach behind Lopez. "We'll knock him out of the box!"

Emmett tried to shut his ears to the racket and concentrate on pitching. He brushed his hand on his trousers, dug in with his cleats, and let it go.

Steve Luke stepped back and caught it near the end of his bat. There was a sharp *crack!* as he connected, and the ball went for a long ride. Ben Kantor sped away from second toward third. The Tiger coach urged him on, and he raced down the base line, crossing the plate on his feet. Steve Luke was not as fast, but he made it to second with plenty of room to spare.

Then Chuck Brislow came from the dugout and started across the field. Al Brown and Hank Winters prepared to join him on the mound, but he waved them back.

"What's the matter, fellow?" he said to Emmett quietly. "It doesn't look like you up here."

"Just having trouble getting in the groove, that's all," Emmett excused himself. "They can't keep it up like this."

"I hope not," Chuck grunted. "You sure you don't want me to take you out?"

It was Emmett's chance, but he shook his head stubbornly. "Watch me this time. They're finished for the inning."

Chuck smiled. "That's the way I like to hear you talk. Go get them!" But Emmett noticed that on his way back to the dugout the grizzled manager motioned to Lou Green in the bull pen. He wasn't taking any chances.

Eddie Bernheim stepped into the rectangle and he had a big, confident grin on his swarthy face. He was a power-puncher with twenty-three home runs on his tally for the season.

Steve Luke was playing it close to second, so Emmett could kill no time there. He was scared for the first time in his life as he faced the Tiger slugger, knowing that if Bernheim hit him, his day would be over and it would be as good as the ball game.

He wiped an arm across his face and shook his head. Right now he would have given all the kewpie dolls in the world for the full use of his right arm, but he was afraid that one hard pitch and he would ruin it for good. And unless he did throw the hard one, Bernheim would tag it sure.

For a moment he had the urge to play it safe and walk him. But Bernheim was only the beginning. He was the leadoff of the Tigers' murderers' row, followed by Schultz, Abraham, and Hano. He couldn't walk all of them!

He flexed his protesting arm and let it go, a slow hook for the outside corner. Bernheim tried to kill it and took a strike. Emmett sighed in relief. It had been close, but if they didn't get any closer he would be satisfied.

The next one was a ball by a foot, followed by still another. Then Hank Winters called for a low outshoot, and Emmett pitched it in.

This time Bernheim waited it out. He watched the ball with squinted eyes and swung solidly, his toes pointed in, his body turned slightly.

As the sphere flew over his head Emmett knew that there was no use watching. It was as good as out of the park, and he was as good as in the showers. He stuffed his glove in a back pocket and started for the dugout as he saw Lou Green coming in from the bull pen.

The Eagles went down 7 to 3, and as Emmett sat in the hotel lobby that evening and read what the scribes had to say he realized that he had given the team a raw deal. The fellows hadn't said anything when they came into the lockers after the game—tired, dirty, and depressed—but their actions had been enough to let him know that they felt the same way about it.

Even Chuck Brislow had given him the treatment. He had said to no one in particular, "I knew it was going to be tough, but not *that* tough. Did we smell!"

Emmett knew that the manager hadn't meant the whole team. They had played their best, running their legs off after the long ones and taking their cuts on deck. The loss was strictly a personal, one-man affair, and the sports writers said as much without mincing words.

Suddenly there was a musical voice saying hello to him, and without looking, Emmett knew who it was. Alice Rivers, the honey-haired blonde with blue eyes who collected kewpie dolls. He felt that he should tell her that she was responsible for what had happened, but then realized it wasn't her fault that he had played the fool. She didn't know about such things. Besides, why go out of his way to hurt her intentionally?

"I couldn't get to the game today," she said slowly, "but I read about it. I don't think the newspapers were fair."

"They were fair, all right," he said. "If Chuck had started Lou Green on the hill we probably would have had at least a chance."

"I waited for your phone call," she said. "When it didn't come I thought maybe it was because of what happened today, and—"

Emmett nodded. "It was."

"—And I hoped I might be able to help cheer you up," the girl finished.

Emmett smiled and took her hand. It certainly wouldn't do his arm any good lounging around in the hotel and brooding. He said, "Let's do something."

Alice beamed at him, her eyes laughing. "Like what?"

Emmett shrugged. "Whatever you like—providing it won't keep me up too late."

She thought a moment, then said brightly, "How about a walk through the park?"

Then went to the park, and at first Emmett enjoyed himself. But after about half an hour he wondered if it had been a good idea. A cool wind was coming in from the river and his shoulder felt chilled. But Alice chattered away gaily as they walked through the darkened paths and he didn't have the heart to tell her about his troubles.

The next morning his shoulder felt worse, and again he knew that he had acted like a fool. If he had stayed in and taken care of himself he might have helped his arm, but now he was right back where he had started the previous day. . . .

In the afternoon Chuck Brislow had Beef McGinnis, the sturdy left-hander, ready for work. His fast one was not as fast as Emmett's, and his hooks and drops did not break with the same abruptness, but he was a steady work horse and could be counted on to turn in a good performance.

Emmett sat in a corner of the dugout, feeling completely washed up. The fans had booed him when he walked out to the field, and their reception had not helped matters. Especially since Alice Rivers had taken the afternoon off to see the game and was up there taking it in.

The Tigers came up and Beef went to work. He fanned Steve Luke and Ben Kantor popped out to Al Brown. Then he walked Les Williams and Joe Gordon got wood on it for a single. Frank Baldwin, Tiger third-bagger, was next up; he sent a grounder bouncing down the first-base line and Bill Lopez scooped it up for an easy out. It was strictly a routine affair, but no tallies were chalked up on the board.

The Eagles came up and were knocked down again. Al Russell was given a free walk, but that was all. Ab Tilton, the Tiger hurler, was really burning them in and the boys couldn't come more than close.

It stayed like that the first two innings, and then the Tigers started to latch on. They collected a walk, two singles, and a double before Beef was able to chop them down.

There was nothing but gloom in the Eagle dugout. The men were already counting it as another loss without trying to fight back.

Al Prescott clouted out a sizzler that should have been a double, but he slammed on the brakes at the turn and backtracked to first. He wasn't in the mood to take a chance. Then Bill Lopez came up and went down again on five pitched balls. Stumpy Lee followed him to the plate and fell nicely into a double play.

They went out again and Chuck Brislow turned anxious eyes on Emmett. "What do you think, fellow?"

"They're not playing. That's easy to see."

"I'm not asking about the other guys," Chuck said. "I mean, what do you think about yourself. Think you can go out there and make like a pitcher?"

Emmett mulled it over for a moment, then said quietly, "I don't know, Chuck."

The manager did not press him further and the game went on. The Tigers brought in another run and when the side was retired the bases were loaded.

"I can't hold them any longer," Beef McGinnis complained when he came in. "They hit everything I toss their way."

It was the signal for a new hurler, and Emmett knew that someone else would have to go to the bull pen.

Chuck grumbled to himself, then turned steady eyes on Emmett. "Get out there and warm up," he ordered in a loud voice.

He went out and the fans booed him all the way. When he reached the pen Chester Lepton, the catcher, said, "Sounds as if they don't like you, chum. I wonder why."

"Could be they don't know the score," Emmett snapped. "Or you either."

"It's right up on the board plain as·day," Lepton returned. "Three for the Tigers, with a nice round doughnut for us."

Phil Phillips, the relief hurler, added, "Well, I hope I can hold them down. Wish me luck."

The Eagles somehow managed to bring in a run

during the frame, Al Brown scoring on a deep one to left field by Gus Foster. That helped things a bit, but then Ab Tilton settled down and tied them up in a neat package.

Emmett tossed a few to Lepton, but he was afraid to burn them in. The twinge was still with him, bringing a stab of pain to his shoulder with every pitch.

Phil Phillips threw a salute as he trotted out to the field and Emmett held up a hand and crossed his fingers. The gesture was for himself as well as Phillips, for if the relief was unable to hold them, Chuck would make another yank and Emmett would be expected to carry the load.

The Tiger tally remained the same for the next two innings, but it wasn't because of Phillips. They hit him unmercifully, and if it hadn't been for perfect fielding it would have been a walkaway. Al Brown on second leaped high into the air to snag one between thumb and forefinger, and Gus Foster climbed the center-field fence to pull down a long one by Eddie Bernheim. A few feet higher and it would have been gone for the day, and the fans gave Foster a rousing cheer.

"Looks like you're next," Lepton said, the sting gone from his voice. "Better limber up that chopper a bit more."

Emmett grunted. "It's as good as it'll ever be." Under his breath he added, "I hope not!"

The Eagles took their cuts without luck, and then they were going out. Chuck Brislow waved Emmett to the mound, and the bull-pen catcher said, "Make it good today, chum. We need this one bad."

Emmett hoped that that wasn't the way they'd get it—bad—but he didn't see any other way. He walked to the center of the diamond, and the fans let him know what they thought of him.

"Here's the bright boy in person!" the Tiger coach yelled from first. "Don't you know when you're licked, guy?"

He tossed a few easy ones to Jack Miller, the chunky backstop who had taken Hank Winters's place behind the plate, and then Les Williams was standing in the rectangle, a grin on his face.

Emmett looked at the stands, wondering where Alice was sitting. A wave from her, he thought, and he would feel better. But he couldn't find her in the milling crowd.

Williams held his bat menacingly and Jack Miller called for the fast one, shoulder-high. Emmett sighed expansively and wound it, wondering how long Chuck would let him stay in.

It was a shade too high but the umpire called it wrong. The Tiger slugger looked at him blackly but did not argue; he was too confident.

Emmett let another one go, and this time it was called right. The count was one and one.

Jack Miller shook his head and signaled for the fireball, jabbing his fingers in anger. But still Emmett was afraid to throw it. He made it a knuckle ball, instead.

It was what Williams had been waiting for, and he

met it squarely. The sphere went deep into right field, but Al Russell somehow pulled it down.

Emmett knew that this was just a carbon copy of the opener. The score still stood at three to one, but he didn't know how long he could hold it there. The way he felt, he was ready to take to the showers right now.

Ab Tilton got up to the plate, crowding it, and a disgruntled Les Williams went back to the dugout, feeling that he had been cheated out of at least a single.

Emmett tried to force Tilton back with an inside pitch, but the Tiger hurler was not fast enough. The ball glanced off his forearm, and another round of catcalls came from the stands as he trotted down the base line.

Steve Luke was next on the list. He selected a bat and walked toward the rectangle, and on the way he waved to someone in the stands. Emmett saw a hand wave back, and suddenly he was burning with anger.

It was Alice Rivers, and she was right over the Tiger dugout!

Now he knew beyond a doubt how big a fool he had been. He had thought that she wouldn't know too much about pitching and arms, that everything had been a coincidence. But now he realized that she was a smart cookie who knew all the angles.

It was all so clever. She had started the whole business in the hotel. She had known about the carnival. She had wanted not one but two kewpie dolls. Then, when he hadn't phoned, she had come looking for him instead of being angry. And she had suggested the walk in the park, too!

Emmett couldn't think of anything except how he had been made a fool of by a pretty smile. Well, he was through being the sucker. He didn't care if he tore his arm off, he wasn't going to let anybody have the laugh on him!

Luke took a grip on his bat and made a couple of practice cuts. He had hit this big Eagle hurler once before and was confident that he could repeat without trouble. He waved his elbows and got set to paste it out. To right field, he thought, but not too deep.

Jack Miller called for an outcurve and Emmett flexed his arm. The twinge was still there but he no longer cared. He put everything he had behind it, and as his arm flashed forward a sharp cry of pain was jerked from between his teeth. He felt something crack in his shoulder, and it almost made him black out.

The ball shot down the alley like a bullet, straight for the Tiger batter. Then it broke at the last moment and rocketed across the outside corner of the plate and smacked into Miller's big mitt with a sharp, satisfying crack. Steve Luke had hit the dirt, and when he got up there was a look of amazement on his face.

Emmett let his arm hang limply at his side. It no longer hurt but he was afraid to move it. The first wave of white-hot anger had passed and now he had no sensation except helplessness.

Miller returned the ball, grinning and shaking his head. Emmett took it mechanically, held it in his glove.

"Now you're cooking, kiddo!" Bill Lopez exclaimed. "Give the bloke some more of the same!"

It had been the kind of pitching Emmett had always

delivered in the past, but he didn't know whether he could do it again. There was only one way to find out. . . .

Emmett put his hands high above his head. But there was no twinge, no hurt. It was just an arm—a good rubber arm that would do anything he wanted it to do!

He felt like standing there and yelling at the top of his lungs. He wanted to tell them that he was all right, again, that he could pitch these Tigers silly. But suddenly he sobered. No one knew that he hadn't been all right all along. They thought he had been shamming for some unknown reason. Well, he would prove he wasn't that kind of a ball player.

Jack Miller indicated another roaster and Steve Luke, the old master, missed by a foot. A swelling yell went up from the fans as the ball steamed into Miller's mitt, and Emmett knew that they were still with him.

He turned to look at Alice Rivers, to see how she was taking this kind of pitching. As he had expected, her face was set in hard lines. She had pulled all the tricks to put him out of the game, and they hadn't worked.

He smiled grimly to himself. Everything that had happened was his own fault, and he knew it. He had been a fall guy for a pretty face and a sweet smile, and it had almost cost his team the series.

But he had learned his lesson; he had learned it only too well. Bold girls and baseball don't mix, and he made up his mind that he'd never go out with another girl if she so much as knew what a baseball looked like.

He took the horsehide again and lifted his hands.

He was going to wrap up this game as soon as possible and get back to the lockers. There was a certain piece of paper in his wallet with Alice's address and telephone number on it, and he wanted to tear it up in little pieces. . . .

Miracle on the Maple

JIM BELL smiled grimly to himself as he climbed the stairs from the lockers in a red and white Trojan uniform. His stunt had worked again, the fifth time in as many basketball seasons, as he had known it would. Just fifteen minutes earlier he had been down to his last thirty-seven cents, and now he was a full-fledged member of the quintet that until a month ago had been a top team in the league.

It had been easy hooking up with the outfit. He had gone up to Shorty Williams, their rotund but tough coach, and said, "My name's Bell. Jim. I'm your new forward."

Williams, sweat shirt over beefy shoulders, whistle around his thick neck on a nickeled chain, had looked him over, from his flaming carrot top to his size-ten bottoms, and had said, "Beat it; we're not in the market."

But Jim had stayed there. He peeled off his shoes and grabbed a ball. He went out on the maple and shot baskets from mid-court. He laced them in from the sides. He trickled them off the backboard with one-hand heaves. Every one had been a bull's-eye, right through the center.

And it had impressed the hard-bitten Williams, just as it had those other coaches. When Jim came off, grinning, Williams said, "Who did you play for last, Bell? I like your style."

Jim rattled off names of clubs, and Williams nodded and jerked a thumb over his shoulder. "Go jump into a uniform. Maybe I can find a spot for you."

But what Jim had failed to mention was the fact that he never stayed more than a season with any one outfit. He had itching feet, and when the call to move on came over him he had to listen to it. This aimless wandering had cost him many a good setup with many a good team, but he had never been able to lick it.

The coach looked Jim over with a cynical eye as he came up on the floor. "Lot of beef you have to carry around," he observed. "Doesn't it slow you down?"

Jim gave him a wide grin. "Give me a chance and I'll show you."

Williams nodded. "O.K. Go in for Downing, with the seconds. But I still want you to take off some of that beef. No fattening foods, understand?"

Time was called and Jim left the side lines. He told the assembled players who he was and a freckle-faced youngster with shaggy blond hair and a scrawny frame beamed at him. "My name's Mike Frohlich," he said. "I saw you two years ago, in Cleveland. You were a ball of fire."

Jim grunted, thankful that Frohlich had seen him at his best. "That was a long time ago; it'll take me a while to get back into condition. Williams just laid the law down about my weight, and he's right."

The first string brought the ball in and started passing it around, looking for a hole. Jim covered his man easily, blanketing him at the side lines. He played slowly, feeling it out to see how his legs would stand up after the layoff. But young Frohlich was all over the court, playing with wild abandon. He had energy to spare, and he snagged a pass and started downcourt in a fast dribble.

The red jerseys rallied and hemmed him in, and he sent it to Jim with a neat backhand. Jim took it on the tips of his fingers, left his feet with a twisting motion, and pushed it at the hoop. The ball whistled through the netting. It gave him a good feeling to know that he could still put them in so easily.

The first string brought it up again, passing cautiously. Ed Parish tried to charge through, then tossed to Stu Hyland. Hyland took his time and let it go. It was good.

Frohlich took the ball out and lobbed to a string bean named Dick Gabriel. Gabriel danced up and passed back to Frohlich and the towhead was away. They boxed him in at the bucket and it was a jump ball.

Mike Frohlich went up after the sphere and deflected it to Jim, and he speared it through the basket without touching the backboard.

They scrimmaged another fifteen minutes and it was five minutes too long for Jim. He was breathing hard and feeling thoroughly bushed by the time Shorty Williams blew the whistle.

"Not bad, Bell, not bad at all," the coach said as they came out. "Stick around, and I'll try to use you against the Bears tonight."

Jim grinned, but he didn't feel happy inside. He had hoped for more time to get into condition, but it seemed that they weren't going to give it to him.

"There's one other thing," Williams said as Jim started down to the lockers. "What do you think of the Trojans? As a team, I mean."

Jim turned, and he saw that Williams was serious. His brow was furrowed and there were little worry lines around his mouth.

"Seem like a good bunch," Jim said. "They should be able to hold their own in any circuit. Why?"

"Just wondering, that's all, just wondering." The coach forced a smile. "Hit the showers and rest up. I'll talk to you later."

Mike Frohlich waited for Jim and they left the arena together. As they walked slowly down the street Mike said, "Where are you staying, Bell?"

Jim shrugged. "I don't have the price of a room."

"There's an extra cot in my place," Mike offered. "You're welcome to it."

Jim said, "Thanks, but I don't know when I'll be able to pay you back."

"Just help the Trojans win," Mike replied quietly, "and we'll call it square. The team has been in the cellar so long I don't know how we'll ever get out."

They came to a sweet shoppe and Jim slowed up. He was still overheated from his workout and his mouth had a dry, blotterlike taste. "How about a plate of ice cream or something?" he suggested. "It'll start the saliva glands flowing again."

The youngster looked at him and frowned. "I

thought you said you had orders to take off some weight. I don't think Williams would like—"

"Look," Jim broke in. "No lectures, please. If you don't want to go in, that's all right with me. But I'm dry. Give me your address and I'll be up later."

But when the sweet shoppe door closed behind Jim he knew that he had been wrong. It was true that he was too heavy to play at his best, and if he was going to be any good for the Trojans he would have to knock off some of those excess pounds. He decided he would give himself a chance.

The following morning as they filed from the lockers Shorty Williams waved Jim aside. He looked closely at the redhead, eyes hard, and said, "I looked up your record, Bell, and it's not good."

This was a new switch on the routine and Jim was caught without a reply. It had always been he who had broken off, and he couldn't afford to get the sack with his finances so low. He turned to go back into the lockers, feeling as if his personal world had collapsed.

"Hold on a minute," Williams stopped him. "All I said was that I looked up your record. But in my book, action on the court means more than newspaper words. Want to give our outfit a chance?"

Jim grinned and started to thank him, but he was glad that he kept his mouth shut. The coach was a tough old codger, and besides, he wasn't finished.

He said, "By the way, that refreshment you had last night is costing you ten bucks; I'll take it out of your check. Now get out there and sweat off some of that beef."

Jim was in a turmoil of emotions as he trotted out to the court. Williams, he thought, was one of the whitest guys he had ever met. Not many coaches will stick their necks out and take a chance on a player with a record. But he had another color for Mike Frohlich. It was clear that Mike had shot his mouth off about the sweet shoppe stop, and Jim didn't like people with loose lips.

Then they were scrimmaging. Slim Atkins, the string-bean center for the red jerseys, took the jump and tapped it back to Stu Hyland. The rangy guard rifled it down to Ed Parish, and the ball whistled through the hoop, a marker in less than four seconds.

Mike Frohlich took it out and lobbed to Gabriel, and Jim went downcourt, dancing for position. Mike took it again on a quick reverse, charged, and passed back to Gabriel. Stu Hyland clipped the guard and Williams blasted his whistle.

"Watch that stuff," he cautioned Hyland. "We're going to need every point tonight, and the Bears will make those fouls count."

They clustered about the basket as Dick Gabriel toed the line. Williams backhanded the ball to him and stepped away. Gabriel bounced it twice and then shot. He took it again, but even as the ball left the guard's hand Jim saw that it was not going to be good. He left his feet in a heave and pushed it back up, to fall through the netting.

When Williams blew the final whistle Jim wasn't quite as bushed as he'd been the previous day. His wind was coming back and it made him feel good. But he had noticed that the fellows had not been feeding them to him, even when he was in the clear, and that he couldn't understand.

He got the answer when he reached the lockers. The rest of the squad was already there, and their eyes were cold. It seemed that Stu Hyland had been appointed spokesman for the team, for the others kept quiet when he walked up to Jim and said:

"Bell, we don't want you with the Trojans. Maybe you've been able to fool Shorty Williams, but we're not so dumb. If you know what's good for you you'll turn in your uniform and beat it."

Jim frowned. "What's the idea? Is it that much of a crime to break training?"

"That doesn't have anything to do with it," Hyland said. "My dad used to work on the Cleveland *Chronicle*, in sports. Phil Hyland. Ever hear of him?"

Then Jim understood. Shorty Williams hadn't said anything to the fellows, but the remark Mike Frohlich had made about seeing him in action in Cleveland had started the ball rolling. Phil Hyland had taken more than a personal interest in the Cleveland Rams, and it was apparent that he considered Jim something of a low-life for pulling out as he had, after only little more than half a season with the outfit.

"All right," Jim said. "I left the Rams because I wanted to. And I'll leave this outfit when I want to—

or when Williams gives me my walking papers. Until then you guys are just wasting your time, get it?"

Hyland nodded curtly. "We get it, Bell. Maybe you'll go on drawing your check every week and maybe you'll wear a Trojan uniform, but don't think that that's enough to put you on the team. As far as we're concerned, you'll be somebody on the floor we never saw before. Do *you* get it?"

He got it all right. They intended to give him the old freeze. They'd play a four-man game out there, and he wouldn't get the ball unless he somehow snagged a pass. With the number of points he'd rack up, it wouldn't take long before he would be let go.

Jim walked around town the rest of the afternoon and early evening. He knew he should have rested, but he didn't want to go to his room. Mike Frohlich would be there, and Jim wanted to stay as far away from him and the rest of the team as he could.

And then it was game time, and Shorty Williams was talking to them in the lockers. His face was a determined mask and he spoke slowly, confidentially.

"Well, this is it," he said. "The third time against the Bears. Think we can take them this time?"

"Sure we can," Mike Frohlich said quickly. "They've beaten us twice, so what? We're better now, and we know their style."

"Besides," Dick Gabriel added, "it'll mean a lot more for us to win now. We need this game to get back in the running."

Williams grinned widely. "That's the way I like to

hear you talk. Let's get going and give them a hot time of it!" He added, "You wait, Bell."

When the squad had filed out Shorty Williams closed the door and leaned heavily against it. He was suddenly old and tired and no longer the tough coach. He walked slowly to the bench where Jim was sitting, sighed, and dropped wearily to it.

Jim didn't know what to expect. Was this just the "talk" Williams had said he was going to have with him, or was it something else? After that scene in the lockers he thought it was probably more logical to expect his first and final pay check from the Trojans and a verbal pink slip.

"So you think the team should be able to hold its own, do you?" Williams said abjectly. "In any league."

Jim sighed to himself. It was the "talk" after all. He said, "That's right. They've got speed, they've got class, and they know how to shoot."

The coach nodded. "Plenty of everything—except on the playing field. Individually they're great, but in action they're strictly second rate. That's the reason I took you on, Bell. You're a floater and I don't like floaters. But you're also a whale of a good, experienced player, and that I need badly."

Jim realized that this would be a good time to keep his mouth shut. He leaned back against the lockers and listened.

"It's worse than I told the boys," Williams said. "A heck of a lot worse." He exhaled sharply and looked at the tips of his fingers, and Jim saw that they were trembling.

"This afternoon," the coach went on, "I got called on the carpet by the men who control the team. They said that we've been losing too many games and too much money. They said that we've become a bad business proposition. They said . . . they said that unless we snap out of it the team is through."

He turned cool, steady eyes on Jim, searchingly. "I'm depending on your basketball know-how to give them the spark they need to push them over the hump, Bell. Think you can do it?"

If it hadn't been so tragic it would have been funny, and Jim didn't know how to answer. The squad had tried to push him out—had virtually blackballed him —and here he was being asked to try to save them!

After a moment he said quietly, "I don't know, Shorty. I can't promise any miracles and I don't even know how to start, but I'll try."

The coach heaved a mighty sigh, the tension gone. "That's enough for me, fellow. Let's get out there now."

Jim stayed on the bench during the first scramble, watching the boys carefully. And he saw what Williams meant. In the opening plays they were like balls of fire, playing brilliantly and romping up and down the court without much trouble. The Bears were a cagewise team and pulled every trick to stop them, but still they forged ahead. Ed Parish and Blackie Hynd tallied two baskets each in the first few minutes, and Stu Hyland accounted for still another. But they were playing without finesse or reliance on their teammates. They scored through their own exuberance and not because of spectacular or even professional ball handling.

As the minutes rolled around the clock the Bears started to tighten up. They played a strong-arm, dazzling game when they got possession of the ball, and the Trojans could not keep up with their passing. Mike Frohlich, who had gone in for Ed Parish, managed to snag a couple, but aside from that the defense was miserable. The Bears started climbing on the scoreboard, and it seemed that the more they closed the score the worse the Trojans became.

Shorty Williams was sweating and it wasn't from the heat of the arena. "If they'd only play like they do in practice!" he exclaimed. "This is murder!"

Jim was also burning with excitement. "Let me go in," he suggested. "Maybe I can sink enough to keep us ahead."

The coach looked at him again with that searching light in his eyes. Then he nodded. "Do what you can, Bell."

Jim trotted out to the floor after the next Bear ringer and the squad greeted him with tight lips and cold eyes. But he ignored the treatment and told Stu Hyland to call time. They got down on the maple and a boy came in with towels.

"Look," Jim said. "You guys don't like me. O.K., we'll let that ride. But you do like the Trojans, and you're going to drop this game down the drain unless you start slinging it around. Pass them crazy and it'll be a walkaway."

"Yeah, sure," Blackie Hynd grunted. "Them over us. What did the coach have to send you in for, anyway?"

"Who are you to hand out orders, Bell?" Stu Hyland said sarcastically. "Go back and warm the bench if you don't like the way things are going."

Jim shrugged, not knowing what else to say. He was trying to give it to them straight but they wouldn't listen to him. He felt that he was letting Shorty Williams down, but he had warned the coach not to expect any miracles, that all he could do was his best.

And he did his best when play was resumed. He raced around the court like a madman. He was everywhere at once, snagging passes, blocking sure points, upsetting plays. He went high into the air and plucked one off the rim of the basket, rifling it to Mike Frohlich before he hit the floor again.

Frohlich was away like a streak, bolting downcourt, and Jim yelled, "Pass it, Mike! Pass!"

But the towhead was deaf. He went into the husky Bear guards and it was a jump ball. Jim saved the play by taking the tap, twisting, and arching it into the net. It was spectacular basketball and brought the first rise from the fans, but it wasn't enough to take the period. At the horn the Trojans were trailing 34 to 36.

Shorty Williams was somber and drawn as he faced them in the lockers. He had very little to say and what he did say was in a whisper, as if he was afraid he'd yell if he raised his voice.

But Stu Hyland had plenty to say. "Coach," he began, "there's not a guy here who wouldn't run his legs off and play his heart out for the squad." He stared squarely at Jim, and amended: "Not a *regular* member of the outfit, that is. We'll do everything you tell us as well as we can. Except one thing. None of us want to play with this Bell joker."

Williams raised his eyebrows quizzically. "What's the matter with Bell?"

"He's no good for the team," Hyland said. "He'll stay for a while and then move on when he gets tired of us. Believe me, I know all about him."

Jim sat back and took it. He couldn't deny anything that had been said, and he knew he would just make a fool of himself if he tried to put up a fight.

But Williams did not see it the same way. He said, "I know all about him too. I know every team he's been with and how long he's stayed with them."

"And you're still going to keep him?" Hyland said incredulously.

"That's right, I'm still going to keep him." The color had started to rise in the coach's face and he was speaking in a clipped voice. "Any objections?"

A look of amazement flashed across Hyland's face. "But I don't understand," he stammered. "Why?"

"Maybe it's because I don't give a hoot about the team," Williams snapped, "and maybe it's because I care a whale of a lot about what happens to it. Take your pick. But if you're not playing ball with Bell you're not playing at all. Is that clear?"

"Plenty clear," Hyland said heatedly. "Maybe that explains why we've been losing so many games lately. How many others are in on this plan to wreck the team, Williams?"

The coach's face was a livid beet-red now but he tried to control himself and said quietly, "Finished?"

"Not yet, I'm not," the big guard retorted. "I'm going to report this to the front office and see what they have to say about it. We'll have another coach here, and quick!" He started peeling off his uniform. "Anybody else going with me?"

Ed Parish, Blackie Hynd, and Slim Atkins got up from the bench and followed Hyland to the other end of the lockers, and Shorty Williams looked over the remainder of the squad with cold, appraising eyes and said, "Now that we're rid of the chaff maybe we can make a real team of this outfit. Or do some of you fellows still think I've been giving you a bum deal?"

Jim said in a low voice, "You can't let them go like that, Shorty. It's your whole team—and for what?"

"For a principle, that's what," Williams said. "All right, now we'll get down to serious work. And I don't mind telling you it's going to be tough sledding out there. The Bears are rugged, but if you'll let me beat some sense into your heads maybe we can still keep from being swamped."

He talked rapidly for the remainder of the half-time, telling them what he wanted to do and how he wanted it done, and then they had to rush up the stairs for the final period.

When they reached the floor Jim said, "You know we don't have a chance, Shorty, with those guys out of the game. It'll be a slaughter."

"I know," Williams said, "but this is one time when I don't care. I'd rather have a bunch of second

strings playing basketball the way it should be played
than a squad of hot-shots who won't learn for sour
lemons. Just do your best out there and I'll be satisfied. Those Bears will know they've been in a fight, anyway."

Hal Adams was at center, but he wasn't tall enough
to take the tap from the bean pole Bear tap-man. He
was greased lightning on the court, though, and stole a
pass before the Bears were able to make their advantage good. He rifled it to Bill Downing, and the shifty
forward who had gone in as a guard let it go to Frohlich on the side lines.

Frohlich was away, bolting downcourt, and passed
to Jim with a skidding bounce. Jim took it up and
dropped it in before the surprised Bears were able to
stop him.

The score was tied up for the moment, but the Bears
soon caught on to the new playing style and altered
their defense. It was then that the difference in experience began to show.

Jim ran himself ragged up and down the court, his
heart pounding, his breath coming faster with each
passing minute. The pace was too hectic for him, out
of condition as he was, but he steeled himself and kept
at it.

The fans in the gallery were getting in the spirit of
the game and started yelling encouragement to the
Trojans. They were for the underdogs now, seeing the
kind of fight they were putting up.

Jim called time after about eight minutes, and when
the squad collapsed to the floor he said, "Well, what do

you think? They're four up on us now, and we've still got a long road to travel."

"We'll keep after them," Bill Downing panted. "Those Bears aren't so tough, and we'll wear them out if we hold this pace."

Jim laughed in spite of himself. He had never heard such optimism, but he liked the way it sounded.

And then Mike Frohlich was talking. He said quietly, "I guess I owe you an apology, Jim. I was riding with Hyland when he told us the story. Especially after seeing you go into that—"

"But you didn't wait long enough," Jim explained. "You see, I decided not to break training after all, figured it would be better to sweat off the beef. O.K., let's get going!"

They started playing again, and it seemed to Jim that the clock on the wall was standing still. The minutes dragged on endlessly, without a letup, and his legs were rapidly turning to rubber. He took a bullet pass from Dick Gabriel and was clipped by a Bear guard before he could shoot. He sighed in relief when the referee blew his whistle and called the penalty.

They grouped around the bucket and Jim took the ball. He looked up at the hoop and it seemed to be wavering. He shook his head violently and blinked his eyes. His reserve was just about gone and he knew he couldn't last much longer.

He took his time getting set, hoping that the basket would stand still. But it didn't and time was running out. He shot once and missed, the first time he'd ever flubbed such an easy one. He took the ball again and bounced it. He held his breath as he flexed his tired arms and let it go. But he could see that it was too short. An orange and black Bear pulled it down, but before he could pass, Mike Gabriel was on him and it was a jump ball.

Jim stood back, knowing that he couldn't take any more fast action. The ball went up and Gabriel tapped it to Frohlich. The towhead flashed away in a fast dribble and made it good with a long oblique shot that brought a gasp from the stands.

The clock said there were six minutes more to go, and Jim knew he'd never make it. He turned anxious eyes to the bench, but Shorty Williams shook his head. There was no one else to send in; Jim would just have to weather it somehow.

"I'm—dead—on my—feet," he gasped to Mike Frohlich after the next Bear basket. "Can't last—much —longer."

"You've got to last, Jim!" Frohlich said anxiously. "They're only three points up, and we need you!"

Jim shook his head numbly. "Can't."

There was no more time to talk. Gabriel passed the ball in and Hal Adams rushed it down the side lines. He shot it to Downing, and after an exchange with Frohlich, Jim saw it coming toward him.

He turned toward the basket somehow, though the backboard was only a white blur, and let it go. Then a Bear defense man bowled into him and sent him spinning.

Jim's body was a throbbing wreck of pain. He felt

the urge to stretch out on the cool maple and go to sleep, but he still had his fighting spirit and struggled awkwardly to his hands and knees.

And then a pair of strong arms suddenly went around him and pulled him to his feet. He couldn't see who it was, but he could feel that the arms were cool and not covered with sweat. He felt himself being half-carried across the floor . . . There was a shouting from the fans—his name . . . And then he was sitting on a bench, his back propped against the wall.

He opened his eyes and shook his head again. Stu Hyland's face swam before him. Only something was wrong. Hyland was smiling, and he was in uniform.

Then Hyland was talking. He said, "Sorry we acted like fools, Jim. We came back to the arena again—for laughs, and to see you guys get licked. But we found out that you and Shorty Williams were right. Anybody with so much guts must be O.K. So now we want to take over from here and wrap this game up. For you, Jim. And for the Trojans."

Jim forced a grin and raised a weary hand. "Good luck, guy," he said, and his mouth felt as if it was filled with cotton fluff.

"Another thing," Hyland went on. "Frohlich didn't tell the coach about that sweet shoppe stop you made. It was my fault—I was walking behind you and Frohlich, and I saw you go in. I'm sorry for that, too."

"Forget it," Jim said. "You were right—I had it coming."

The big forward took Jim's hand in his, pressed it

warmly. Then Hyland's face abruptly disappeared, to be followed by the sound of a whistle and running feet.

A cool towel was wiped across Jim's face, and then he heard Shorty Williams's excited voice. "You did it, Bell! You turned those bums into real hoopsters! A miracle!"

Jim leaned back and closed his eyes. He was completely fagged out but he'd never felt so good. Yes, he told himself, the Trojans were all right. They should be able to hold their own in any league. He thought he'd stick around as long as they would have him. He thought he'd enjoy that. He thought he'd enjoy it a whale of a lot!

ROD CAMPBELL swung the all-white and gleaming *Beane Special* into the wind and cranked down the landing gear. Easing the stick forward, he went into an approach glide, blipping the in-line, air-cooled Menasco engine in the streamline nose of his racer to keep it from conking out. He leveled off a few feet above the runway, chopped the throttle all the way back, and slowly hauled the stick into his stomach.

The wheels touched, bounced, and settled again. Without flaps, the *Beane Special* had a hot landing speed and anything less than three bounces was considered a perfect landing.

Satisfied that the *Special* should be able to take the Guy Gundelach Trophy and purse money without trouble, Rod taxied up to the line and slowly swung into position with the other aerial speedsters entered in the annual classic. He cut the switch, locked the parking brake, and reached up to open the transparent bubble canopy.

Doug Beane, owner, builder, and chief mechanic of the *Special,* a worried look on his face, was waiting when Rod stepped from the wing root to the ground.

"How did it go, boy?" he asked anxiously. "Everything in order?"

Rod had become accustomed to the old pilot's constant anxiety over the condition of the ship, and he said, "How do you want the purse money, cash or check? It's as good as yours already."

Doug almost smiled, but not quite. "Think she's good enough to beat the *Messner Master?*" he asked.

That was something Rod did not know. After the previous year's race Lloyd Messner had announced that he was going to put his crack engineers to work on a ship to be entered in the next running of the event. The speedster had made its first test flights only two weeks ago, and Messner had issued some spectacular performance claims. The only consolation was, he had not been satisfied with his pilot talent and was looking around for the right man to handle the *Master*.

Rod shrugged, unconcerned. "Why worry about a ship that's not even entered? We can take the ones we know are going to be in the race, and that's all that counts."

"The Messner will be in there too," Doug said quietly. "It came in while you were up there tooling around."

Rod had a strange sinking sensation. He had been afraid of the *Master* even though he had never seen the ship, and had hoped she wouldn't be entered. For no matter how good a homemade plane might be, built in a garage and with limited funds, it was hard to believe that such a ship could take the measure of a custom-made machine put together by the best aeronautical brains.

"And Walt Saxon will be at the stick," Doug added.

It was a double blow to Rod: the *Messner Master* and Walt Saxon. One without the other would have been bad enough, but combined they would make a team hard to beat.

He remembered without pleasure the association he'd had with Saxon during World War II, when they were both on P-47 Thunderbolts in the Eighth Air Force. Saxon had been the Group's leading ace, and he never let the other fellows forget for a minute that he was the squadron commander and gave the orders.

Rod had had the dubious distinction of being Saxon's wingman—the work horse who stayed behind and watched for trouble while the Great One blasted more Jerry ships out of the air and built his score ever higher.

Rod had saved Saxon's life on more than one occasion, but the ace had never given him any thanks. On one sweep, a fighter-bomber mission to the Renault factory outside of Paris, a flight of snub-nosed Focke-Wulf Fw. 190's had jumped them from low-hanging clouds. It had been close for a few hectic minutes, trying to fight at such a low altitude, and two of the Nazis converged on Saxon.

But Rod had been alert, and he knocked down one of the Focke-Wulfs and chased the other one off. He had left himself wide open from the rear while making the attack, but it had saved Saxon from digging a sure grave for himself.

When they returned to their base Saxon had expressed his appreciation in a peculiar way.

"You almost rammed me, you fool," he said heatedly. "Try anything like that again and I'll blast you out of the sky with my own guns!"

But there was no denying that Saxon was a great pilot. He could jockey a fast plane with smooth precision and judge distance to the fraction of an inch. Regardless of what Rod thought about the man personally, he knew that Saxon would be a tough one to beat, especially when toying the stick of a perfect job like the *Messner Master*.

Doug Beane studied his pilot's face, his eyes clouded with concern. "Well, can you or can't you beat him?"

Rod shrugged. "How can I answer that? I know the kind of stuff the *Special* packs under her cowling, and I know she will make all those other crates look like they're standing still. But I haven't even seen the Messner job."

"Then take a good look," Doug said, pointing with a callused finger. "They're just rolling her this way."

Rod looked, and he didn't like what he saw. He didn't like the idea of having to race against it, that is. Painted a dazzling gold and black, the *Master* appeared to have been molded, it was so perfect. A sleek mid-wing with smoothly tapered panels, it was streamlining personified from the tip of its exaggerated prop boss to a tail section that grew gracefully from an oval empennage.

As they drew closer he could see that the ship would create almost no drag at all. The rivets were flush with the Alclad skin, and even the tail wheel was retractable to cut resistance to a minimum.

But above everything else, he didn't like the sight of the figure at the wing tip. It was Walt Saxon, and he was dressed in coveralls to match the *Master's* pretentious finish.

"It's the ace in person," Doug said. "Aren't you going to say hello to him?"

Rod grunted. "Why should I?"

Doug stared at him, puzzled. "I thought he was a friend of yours. You flew with him during the war, and—"

"And I hate his insides," Rod interrupted. "I don't want any part of him. Come on, let's get out of here."

But Saxon had seen them too, and he left the *Master's* wing tip and came toward them, smiling. He had grown a mustache since the war, Rod saw, and it somehow made him appear even more sardonic.

"Hello, Campbell," said Saxon. "I understand from hangar gossip that your crate is the only one that can give me any competition."

"Maybe," Rod said. "We'll find out when we get up there."

"You must be Beane," the ace said to Doug. "No offense meant, but the *Master* and I are going to walk away from your entry. It'll be just like the old days: Campbell will be flying wingman for me again."

Saxon's blunt approach did not bother Rod; he had become accustomed to it during the war and learned to ignore the sarcasm. But not so Doug Beane. He got red in the face and started breathing heavily.

"Yes, I'm Beane," he bellowed. "But you're not going to walk away from anybody. Not my plane, anyway!"

Saxon smiled and said quietly, "Want to make a little bet?"

"You're darn right I do," Doug said. "Anything—"

"Wait a minute," Rod broke in quickly. "Don't lose your head, Doug."

"Keep out of this, Campbell," Saxon said evenly. Then, to Doug, "How about a thousand dollars?"

Doug faltered for a moment, staggered by the figure, and Saxon needled him with, "What's the matter, are you yellow, Beane? It'll be a pushover—if the *Special's* as good as you think she is."

"It's a bet," Doug whispered, his voice hoarse. "We'll settle up right after the race."

Later, in the field's coffee shop, Rod said, "Why did you make such a crazy bet, Doug?"

"The flap-jaw got me sore," Doug replied, stirring his coffee nervously. "You'd think he owns the sky, the way he talks."

"Suppose we lose?"

"Don't even think about it. We've *got* to win."

"But we have to think about it," Rod insisted. "It wouldn't mean so much if you hadn't made that bet, but if we lose now you'll have to pay up. And what are you going to use for money?"

"You sound like you think it's already lost."

"I'm trying to be practical," Rod said. "We haven't got a thousand dollars between us, and you know it. If we drop the race you'll have to sell the engine out of the *Special* to pay Saxon!"

Doug shook his head and, changing the subject, said, "Are you flying again this afternoon?"

"Yes," Rod sighed, "I guess so. There are a couple more things I want to check, just to be sure. And maybe I can get a few more revs out of her with an intake adjustment. We'll probably need them tomorrow if the going gets tough."

The Guy Gundelach Trophy Race was run over a triangular course thirty miles long, with three pylons and ten-mile legs. On the morrow Rod would cut those checkered markers as close as possible without swinging inside, but now he had other things more important to do. Flying at about 5,000 feet, he was checking the revs on the Menasco engine in the nose, making fine adjustments to squeeze better performance from the little ship.

An all-red pusher pulled up next to him. Tony Randolph was at the stick, and he made a hand motion challenging Rod to an individual race.

Rod waved back and shook his head. He knew that the *Special* could beat Randolph, but there was no use proving it to everybody else.

A few minutes later another ship took the pusher's place. It was the *Messner Master,* and the gold-helmeted figure in the cockpit made the same challenge.

Rod said no again, and then suddenly he was bursting with anger. Saxon was pointing upstairs and to the rear with his thumb, as he had done during the war to tell Rod to fly top cover for him. But this time Rod wasn't taking it. He knew that Saxon had made the gesture in ridicule, and he was through taking that kind of treatment.

He hit the throttle savagely with the heel of his hand, and the *Special* roared alive. The tach needle climbed around the dial, and at the turn they were even.

Rod shaved the pylon close in a vertical bank, the stick in his stomach. He noticed with satisfaction that the *Special* could make a tighter bank than the *Master*, and he pulled away from the gold and black creation.

But not for long. The engineering work that had gone into the Messner speedster became apparent on the straightaway, and it slowly closed the gap.

Rod slapped the throttle against the backstop and made another adjustment, trying to coax more speed out of the Menasco, but it wasn't enough. The *Master* crept ahead inexorably. It wasn't a great deal faster than the *Special*, but enough to make the difference between winning and losing. At the turn it had opened the gap to about thirty yards.

Rod yanked his little racer around the pylon in a screaming bank, and it was tight enough to put him ahead again. But once more the *Master* closed the distance and roared into the lead, and Rod knew that he would never be able to win the Gundelach Trophy. The *Special* was good, but not quite good enough.

After the duel Rod came in with a feeling of defeat. Everything he and Doug Beane had worked and slaved for was going to be bowled over just because of the egotism of one man. Lloyd Messner was a wealthy manufacturer and did not need the purse money. He wanted to win only to prove his superiority, and for no other reason. His plant wouldn't even profit by research data from the *Master*, because the little ship was not much more than a toy when compared with the jet fighters and bombers he was turning out for the Air Force.

Doug Beane's usual worried look was more pronounced as he helped Rod climb from the *Special's* narrow cockpit. But he did not say anything about the race against Saxon. He took a rag from his pocket and started wiping oil streaks from the cowling.

Rod said quietly, "You saw what happened up there?"

Doug nodded. "He's got a faster ship."

"It skids badly on the turns. Can't hold a tight bank as well as the *Special.*"

"But it's faster," Doug said again. "Just enough to take the flag."

"And a thousand dollars we haven't got," Rod added. Then, quickly, "Do you have a saw?"

Doug lowered his rag and looked at Rod quizzically. "What do you want a saw for?"

"I'm going to slice about a foot off each wing panel."

Doug shook his head. "You're crazy. She would be too hot to land."

"Don't worry about landing," Rod said. "I'll get her down somehow. But we've got to cut down the wing and throw out every bit of weight we can. It's our only chance, Doug, you know that."

The little owner sighed and nodded. "I was thinking the same thing when I saw Saxon walk away from you up there, but I didn't want to make the landing speed too hot."

"Then what are we waiting for?" Rod exclaimed. "Let's roll her into the hangar and get to work."

"We don't have enough time," Doug said. "I couldn't do it by myself and have her finished for the race, and you've got to get plenty of sleep tonight."

"Forget about the sleep," Rod said in annoyance. "I can sleep for a week after the race. Come on, let's get started."

It was an easy job cutting off the wing tips, but tapering the stubs and adding new covering was a different matter. They worked through until after three o'clock in the morning, and when they were finished the *Special* had been stripped of all extra equipment, including the plastic knob on the throttle and the rubber grip on the joy stick.

"There she is," Doug said at last, wiping his hands on a ball of waste. "An engine with wings and not much else. If we stripped her down any more she would probably fall apart."

"But she should be good for another ten miles per hour," Rod said tiredly. "Maybe even more."

"And twenty to thirty higher on the landing speed," Doug added, his brow creased with concern. "It will be just like sitting on a bullet."

That night Rod had trouble sleeping. Ordinarily the tension of racing did not bother him, but this time there was too much to fight for. Now it meant more than just a race; it meant the difference between gaining the purse and losing the plane.

And Walt Saxon's presence in the race bothered him

more than he had admitted even to himself. You have to keep a cool head on your shoulders when racing on a tight course, but Rod did not see how he would be able to keep cool with Saxon flying so close to him.

Doug Beane was already at the field the following day when Rod arrived, and his worried expression was deeper than ever.

"I can't let you do it, Rod," he said. "I sat up figuring it out last night, and my calculations show that the *Special* will land at almost one fifty. That's too fast for such a little ship."

"Forget it," Rod said, grinning. "Let's tune up the motor and get ready to give that Messner job a real race."

While they worked the stands filled, and the program got under way. Air Force F-94C jets started it with a demonstration of high-speed formation and stunt flying. Then came the parachutists, spot landings, and short races for low-powered personal planes. Then Major Al Grey put on a display of aerobatics in his red and white Conch Oil Special, and it was time to run the Guy Gundelach Trophy Race.

Right before the call came, Walt Saxon walked up and ran his eyes over the Beane racer. "Looks like you've been working," he observed. "Do you think this tub is fast enough to beat the *Master* now?"

Doug looked at the ace coldly. "I know so, Saxon. Rod will run you out of the race."

Saxon smiled knowingly. "I'm glad you've got a good sense of humor, anyway. But I wasn't kidding when we made that bet."

"Maybe you'd like to make it a little more," Doug said impulsively, his temper running away with him.

The ace's eyes seemed to light up. "Suits me fine. How about another thousand?"

"I've got a better idea, Saxon," Rod said before Doug could answer. "Suppose we make it that if you win I drop out of racing for keeps, and if I take the flag you fade from the picture. Are you game?"

Saxon's face split in a grin. "Perfect, shavetail! It's a bet."

After the ace had gone, to taxi the Master out to the take-off line, Doug shook his head sadly. "It will be bad enough losing the *Special*," he said slowly, "but you shouldn't have made a bet like that."

Rod pulled a helmet on his head. "Why not? You can find pilots at any airfield, but there's only one *Beane Special*. I had to try to save the plane for you somehow, before you gave it to the guy as a present."

Then it was time to go, and Rod climbed into the cockpit and Doug spun the prop. The Menasco caught, sucking in raw gas, coughed a few times, and blasted to life with a throaty roar. Rod listened to it for a few seconds, nodded, and made a thumbs-up gesture to Doug Beane. Doug held up both hands, fingers crossed for luck.

But Rod did not feel so well as he acted. He hadn't tried the revamped *Special* before because he was a little afraid of it, with the wings clipped so short. Doug had figured a landing speed of almost one fifty, and that meant he would have to hit at least twenty or thirty miles more to take off with full control. That was a healthy speed for any plane, and a big handful for a ship as small as the *Special*.

He took his place in line and paraded slowly in front of the stands, while the announcer at the public address system introduced the pilots and said something about the planes entered. And then they were backtracking to the end of the field, waiting for the signal to take off.

Then came the signal, and the field became a bedlam of thunder and vibration. Rod kept his eyes straight ahead, holding the *Special* on a perfect line, constantly inching the throttle ahead.

The air speed indicator climbed to 100—125—140 —and still she wasn't light enough to leave the ground with full control. The field was being used up fast, the trees at the end of the runway growing larger. Then, at the last moment, he eased the stick back. The little ship lifted, faltered slightly, and then climbed sluggishly away.

Rod sighed with relief, and quickly cranked up the landing gear. The long take-off had dropped him back to fourth position, but now he was no longer worried.

He shot past a cream-and-blue job before the first pylon turn, and in the bank he swung inside of Tony Randolph's crimson pusher. Tony waved him on, and he inched the throttle ahead. He was thankful that the other pilots had not opened up at the start, giving their engines more time to warm. But he knew he didn't have to worry about the *Special* conking out; Doug had adjusted her too carefully for that.

They were still climbing at the second turn, and

Walt Saxon was only a hundred yards in the lead. The real race would begin when they reached 1,000 feet, and from the way the *Special* was handling, Rod thought he would have a very good chance of taking the *Master*'s measure before the five laps had been completed.

He held tight to the second pylon, his ears popping from the strain of the vertical. But the shortened wing panels did not skid and he picked up another thirty yards, still slowly closing the gap.

Then the altimeter read an even 1,000 feet and Rod tensed himself. The *Special* had proved that she could climb like a rocket, but the straightaway was something else again.

He pushed at the throttle, but it was tight against the backstop. The Menasco up front was turning over at maximum revs and would not make one turn faster. He was still creeping up on the gold-and-black job, but he couldn't tell if Walt Saxon had opened her up all the way.

He got his answer at the next pylon, the end of the first lap.

Slamming his left wing down hard and yanking back on the stick, Rod pulled up even with the *Master*. They tore along spinner to spinner, and then Saxon looked at him and grinned. He jerked a thumb up and back as he had done the previous day—and slowly pulled away! He had held a little extra power in reserve, and the *Special* could not match it!

Rod yelled above the roar of his engine and beat a balled fist against the throttle. Lloyd Messner's precision-built ship was going to win out after all, and there was nothing he could do about it. The only chance he had was that Saxon would be forced from the race by engine trouble. But he knew that was not likely, that the *Master* had been tuned just as perfectly as the *Special*.

He flew a crazy, relentless race, clinging tenaciously to every foot. He didn't touch the throttle even in the whip turns, and almost blacked out once from the draining pull as he swung around a pylon.

No pilot in his right mind would have flown such a race, but Rod was not in his right mind. The thought continued to pound into him with every turn of the crankshaft that if he didn't win, the *Special* would have to be junked to pay the bet with Saxon. It would be the end of everything Doug Beane had lived for, and with the skids under him he would never be able to come back in the game.

But the *Master* did not pull ahead any farther, Rod noted with satisfaction. He opened the gap to about two hundred yards on the straightaway, but at the pylons the shorter turn of the *Special* cut it down again to less than a hundred and fifty yards. It would be close at the finish, but not close enough.

At the end of the third lap they were still in the same positions, with the other ships remaining in the race strung out far to the rear. The two tail-enders had dropped, seeing that they had no chance at all. The others stayed in only because they knew that anything can happen in air racing, and generally does.

Rod laughed without humor when he sliced another

twenty yards from the gap as the *Master* slipped wide on a turn.

"I'm still in the race, Saxon," he yelled into the slip stream. "Let's do that a few more times!"

But the ace did not repeat. He pulled it tighter at the pylons, if anything, and held his position without wavering.

Suddenly, as they hit the last turn of the third lap, Rod got an idea. No minimum altitude had been set for the race and he thought he knew a way to win. It was worth a try, anyway—the only thing he had left in his bag of tricks.

He held close to Saxon's tail, trying to cut the distance every inch to give his plan more chance. They rounded one turn . . . two . . . and then it was the last turn and a ten-mile straightaway to the chalk line.

Rod righted the controls quickly as he came out of the turn and then pushed forward on the stick, putting the *Special* into a shallow dive. He increased the angle, letting gravity pull him down and add more speed to the ship. As the angle steepened he cut back on the throttle to keep the whirling propeller from acting as a brake.

The trees at the end of the field grew larger and blacker, but Rod kept his nose pointed straight at them. He shot a glance up at the *Master* and saw that the gap was smaller. He was breathing rapidly, his nerves on edge, and he could hear his heart above the growl of the engine.

The trees were now right in front of him, too close

for safe flying, and Rod quickly leveled out and at the same time hit the throttle all the way forward.

The engine pounded and strained, gulping in the fuel, and the *Special* shot forward at a greater speed than it was ever meant to attain. The stands on the right were a blur of screaming faces, and the field was only feet under his fuselage. He was rhubarbing it as they had never taught him in the Air Force.

A hundred yards from the finish line he was even with the *Master*. Saxon had seen the trick and was also diving. But he had started the dive too late, and the *Special* rocketed across the chalk, winning by a good twenty yards!

Rod let out a shout as he got the flag, and then corkscrewed straight up in a wild roll. He had done the impossible. He had beaten the fastest ship in its class by remembering that Rudy Kling had once come from behind at the Cleveland Air Races by pulling the same stunt—diving to build up enough speed to come out the winner.

After a few minutes of stunting, Rod calmed down and made a wide sweep around the field. He still had to land the *Special*, and from what Doug Beane had said, that was not going to be easy.

He made a long approach, judging his glide carefully, and touched trucks with the engine turning over fast, flying it in instead of stalling. He flashed down the runway on his main wheels, slowly cut the throttle, and trod the brakes. The tail came down and he held back on the stick, slapping the brakes hard and at the same time gunning the engine to keep from nosing over. The *Special* mushed to a stop not more than fifty yards from the end of the concrete strip.

Doug Beane had the canopy open and was screaming unintelligibly even before Rod switched off. The worried look was gone from his face and he was laughing like a child with his first piece of candy.

"You did it, you crazy fool, you did it!" he exclaimed. "You beat the *Master!*"

"I know," Rod laughed. "But control yourself. You'll have a stroke at this rate."

"Lloyd Messner is here today," Doug raced on. "He wanted to see his ship win. He—he offered me a job—a good job—in his plant, after seeing you win."

Rod quickly sobered. "What did you tell him?"

"I told him to go chase himself. What did you think?"

Rod lifted himself from the cockpit, smiling again. "I think we ought to go collect on that bet," he said, "before Saxon gets any bright ideas about pulling out. Come on, let's find the fallen ace!"

The Big Diamond Feud

CLEVE BREWSTER was a tall, slope-shouldered man with powerful arms, big hands, and legs that were sturdy and solid. His face was a weatherbeaten reddish-brown that would never fade, and around his eyes were deep crow's-feet earned by squinting into the sun for too many years. Everything about him labeled him as a ball player.

There was only one thing wrong, and that was the color of his close-cropped hair. It was no longer a deep, shining black, but was slowly turning iron gray. By insurance company life expectancy charts he was still a young man at thirty-eight, but for baseball he was well past his prime.

That was why he had not understood the telephone call he had received from Pat Garver, leather-lunged manager of the Wolves. Pat had called him at his upstate farm the previous evening, his voice anxious, asking him to come down as soon as he could.

"Sure, fellow, sure," Cleve had said. "I'd like to see the bunch again, but what's it all about? I can't just pick up and—"

"Tell you when you get here," Pat had cut him off. "But believe me, it's important. Throw a couple of clean shirts in a bag and hop on the first train out. See you tomorrow. Good-by."

Cleve hadn't known what to do. When he retired

from the Wolves two years ago he knew he would never be able to return to their stadium again. He had made a clean break—had tried to, anyway—to save himself heartaches.

But now, in answer to the telephone call, he was seated in the Wolves' business office, and Pat Garver was on the other side of the mahogany desk, a cigar in his mouth.

The team's pilot was shorter than Cleve, and heavier. But there wasn't an ounce of fat under his skin. Pat Garver was as lean as a mule steak and just as sinewy. He had a pugnacious chin, a nose that had been flattened far in the past by a hard-pitched ball, and beetle brows which met in a great hairy tangle.

"It's been a long time, fellow," he said in a husky voice. "Too darn long, if you ask me. Let's see—it's been about two years, right?"

Cleve nodded. Two years on the calendar. But it seemed like two hundred, time had dragged so heavily. He had tried to cultivate a hobby up on the farm to pass away the hours of inactivity, but even that had not helped. Every time he locked a piece of wood into his lathe and turned it down, it somehow became a baseball bat instead of a table leg.

Pat said, "Ever think about the old days?"

"They're just about the only things I do think about," Cleve admitted. "But what good does it do me? I'm a has-been hurler and I know it. Maybe I used to have steam in my arm, but the fire has gone out."

Pat took the cigar from his mouth, looked at it

thoughtfully, and then tapped ashes toward the paper basket.

He said quietly, "How would you like to come back to the outfit?"

Cleve smiled ruefully. "As maybe a trainer or ticker hawker? No thanks! If you got me down here just for that, you're wasting your time."

"I mean," Pat said, "to pitch."

Cleve laughed. "You're kidding, I hope."

"But I'm not," Pat said seriously. "We've needed you a lot these past two years, but right now we need you more than ever."

Cleve thought about it for a moment. He would feel good getting back into uniform again, but he knew that it was too much to hope for. Pitchers never came back out of retirement, and he didn't think that he would be the exception.

"Sorry, Pat," he said, shaking his head, "but you're wasting your time. It's just no good."

"It has to be good!" exclaimed the fiery manager. "We got the skids pulled from under us all at once. First it was Bob Doolin with chips on the arm, and then Walt York tried to stop a drive and wound up with a broken finger. Lou Fisher got a bad dose of spikes in his leg covering first, and then yesterday Al Thaw came up with an arm so lame he couldn't pitch spitballs. It's a bad streak of luck, and here we are going down the stretch only a game from first place!"

Cleve said, "It's tough, but what can I do about it?"

"You can get out there where you belong and toss

them," Pat said. "But I'm not asking you to do it, see —I'm telling you."

Cleve smiled. "You mean it's an order?"

"That's right, it's an order. Maybe you think you resigned from the Wolves, but I never signed your release. We've just been letting you rest up there on that farm."

Cleve's smile had become a wide grin. "Well, if that's the way it is," he said, "I guess there's not much I can do about it."

"Now you're talking sense," Pat said, his voice suddenly warm again. "I knew you'd listen to reason."

"Or get my teeth kicked in," Cleve added, jokingly. "But seriously," he said, "I think you're making a mistake. Maybe I can still hook a few and put them where I want them, but one fast one and my arm will go down the chute with it. I'm a lot older, Pat, and age doesn't wear so well out there on the mound."

"But it makes a guy settle down and puts a head on his shoulders. And that's what this club needs—players with more head and less mouth. Now go climb into a uniform," he said in a stern voice. "You'll find one in your old locker. And snap it up, because I'm going to work the blazes out of you."

Cleve felt like a raw rookie going to the lockers for the first time. His heart was thumping harder than it should have been, and he had to swallow to keep a lump from forming in his throat. He remembered he'd had the same reaction that day so many years ago when he came up to the Wolves full of wild stories about how rookies were treated in the big time.

But now it was worse. A lot of things can happen to the line-up of a ball team in two years, and there would be faces of fresh, eager kids—kids who had energy to spare and who wouldn't want to be held back by an old man with half an arm.

He swallowed again and pushed on the door. Players he had never seen before were sitting on the benches in various stages of dress, laughing and swapping jokes. As he passed by, two or three of them looked at him briefly without recognition and then turned away again. Cleve felt like a stranger in his own back yard.

He tried to find some of the old-timers, but none were in sight. He sighed and went to his locker, spinning the dial on the combination without even having to think of the numbers. Then he opened the door—and bedlam broke loose.

A bucket above the locker tipped over and drenched him with chilling water, a bugle blared in raucous discord, a string of firecrackers went off, and in the background came the loud, unmusical sound of untrained voices singing "For He's a Jolly Good Fellow."

And then, suddenly, a dozen hands were pounding on him and he saw the homely, laughing faces of his old squad.

There was Little Reed Little, the lanky short fielder; Tom Jervey, the first-sacker with arms so long he could snag a heave ten feet away; laughing Fred Veil, the keystone man who had once raced a horse around the diamond and won; Don Parks, Art Kelly, and Bill Hassinger, the three greatest power-punchers in the league; and rotund Earl Richards, the sleepy thirdsacker who could belt them a mile when his bat was in shopping trim.

"The prodigal son returns!" laughed Little Reed Little. "Just look at those gray hairs, will you!"

"That's just rust from the iron in his head," joked Tom Jervey. "The bum's falling apart."

"Naw," Art Riley put in. "It's dust from that farm of his. He doesn't get enough baths."

"Then what are we waiting for?" yelled Little Reed Little. "Let's get him in the showers!"

Laughing like a pack of kindergarten youngsters, they half-dragged, half-carried Cleve into the showers, clothes and all, and turned on the water. Tom Jervey was wearing a neat pin-stripe suit with fresh creases, but he didn't let it bother him. He stood under the spray, singing loudly, and rubbed Cleve's head with a cake of soap while the others kept him from squirming away.

They were all soaked and dripping when Don Parks at last shut off the tap, but they were also happy.

"That'll teach you," said Bill Hassinger. "The next time you pull any stuff about leaving the team you'll get the same thing all over again. Only it'll be your whole body, and with a steel-wire brush!"

"O.K., O.K.," Cleve laughed. "I give up. I'll stay till this arm of mine falls off."

"Then put it here," said Little Reed Little, extending a big hand. "Glad to have you back where you belong."

Cleve shook hands all around, and then said, "But

I'm not forgetting this, you bums. For ruining my suit, I'm going to pitch you silly when we get out there."

But Pat Garver wouldn't let him try it right away. "You haven't done any heaving for a long time," he said when Cleve came out to the field. "Take it easy for a while, and warm up with Joe Newell. Then, if your arm feels all right, I'll let you try a few on the mound."

So he took it easy, throwing nothing-balls without sting for a good half hour, just to get the feel of the sphere in his hand. But actually he had never lost the feel, he realized as he tossed them in. Those two long, dismal years on the farm had been pushed to the back of his mind, and as far as he was concerned he had never left the Wolves.

After he was thoroughly limbered, the arm greased and working smoothly, he powdered in a few riding behind a little juice, and they plunked into Joe Newell's glove with a satisfying *thwack!*

"Hey, I thought you were supposed to be on crutches!" said Newell, a newcomer to the outfit. "They're riding in real nice, buddy. Real nice?"

Such a compliment made Cleve feel even better, though it wasn't completely true. He knew that he wasn't putting enough power behind them, but it was all he had. They were breaking right and hitting Joe's glove, but still they were a great deal tamer than the kind he had once thrown. That old fireball, he knew, was one thing he could never get back.

"O.K., fellow," Pat Garver said at last, "get up there

and see what you can do. I'll back you up and watch them break."

Don Parks was first up, and he had a grin on his face and a bat in his hands as big as a telephone pole.

"Just put 'em in, Grandpaw," he taunted good-naturedly, "and I'll slam 'em for you. Let's go!"

Cleve's heart was thumping again. This was the real test, and he knew it. For the Wolves as well as for himself. They needed each other to go on living, but he would never let himself be deadwood to the outfit.

Pat Garver called for a low one on the inside, and Cleve wound it slowly and let go. The ball seemed to float to the plate, breaking at the last moment before cutting across the inside corner. Don had his eye on it and let fly with a mighty punch.

But something went wrong. He missed and the ball clumped into Pat Garver's big mitt.

"That's the way to do it," Pat yelled from behind his mask. "Keep it up, kiddo!"

Cleve wound up again with new confidence, and again Don Parks plugged at it and missed. He blooped the next one foul, and Pat waved him away from the plate after the fourth pitched ball.

"And him complaining he's in a wheel chair!" Don growled, throwing down his bat. "What does that make me, I wonder?"

Kelly was next up, and he went down again swinging, without even getting a piece of it. And then Bill Hassinger stepped into the rectangle.

"Twice, maybe," the slugger avowed, "but not three times. Watch your hat on this one, Cleve!"

But he didn't do any better than the others, and Cleve frowned darkly. It was impossible that he could be whiffing such power-punchers without his old fast one. Somehow it just didn't add up, and he didn't like the way the pieces were piled. He hadn't been able to do this well even in the old days when he'd had the steam to press them back. It was too easy.

And then he thought he understood. These men were his friends. Probably the best friends he'd ever had. And they were wearing their hearts on their sleeves. They were deliberately missing, so that he would look good to Pat Garver. That had to be it!

He decided to find out, and said, "Put up one of the newer boys, Pat. Let's see if I can do as good with them."

The little manager nodded and waved to a string bean named Jim Lunt. The youngster was new this season and his uniform was still clean. He didn't know Cleve and didn't owe him anything, and would do everything he possibly could to rip the horsehide off the ball. Which was just the way Cleve wanted it.

Lunt was a southpaw and he crowded the plate, cleats towed in, wrists flexed, body turned slightly. His eyes were cool and steady, and he watched carefully as Cleve wound the pitch.

It went down the alley like a slow freight, letter-high, spinning stitches making a crazy pattern of color. Lunt tracked it in, bat poised, muscles tensed, trying to judge the break. And Cleve held his breath, his heart thumping in his ears.

The slugger swung, leaning back, snapping his

wrists for more power, and there was a sharp *crack!* that broke Cleve's spirits. The ball took wings and arched straight out toward center field, mounting higher and higher. It came down in a long, graceful sweep and bounced high off the fence.

That was the ticket, Cleve knew. The first ball in and Lunt had clouted it. Which meant that the old-timers had actually been giving him a free ride.

And he also knew that he had been right the first time. Pitchers never come back out of retirement. The trail is there, all right, but it's too steep for an old man to climb.

After the workout Tom Jervey loaned Cleve a suit of dry clothes and he climbed into them silently. The boys were talking it up as they always did, but Cleve stayed out of it. He had his own thoughts and they weren't pretty to visualize. After having his hopes raised so high, he knew that it would be back to the farm again. And this time it would be worse, because he would know for sure that he was a has-been, without a chance of coming back to the only thing he wanted to do.

Pat Garver, another cigar in his mouth, was working over some papers when Cleve went into his office. He looked up briefly and smiled.

"Nice job you did out there, fellow," he said. "Not perfect, of course, but nice. I'm starting you tomorrow against the Sox."

Cleve shook his head slowly. "Better make it somebody else," he advised. "I'm not going to hang around."

Pat sat back in his chair, eyes hard, and stared at

Cleve unbelievingly. "What are you talking about?" he demanded. "I thought we had that all out."

"So did I," Cleve said quietly. "But Jim Lunt changed everything. I can't do it, Pat, without my fast one."

"Nonsense!" Pat roared. "He got a piece of it, so what? You think any pitcher is so perfect he can fan everybody? You're back on the squad again, so let's drop it."

But Cleve wouldn't drop it. "I'm taking the train out tonight," he said. "There's no use trying to argue."

The fire suddenly went out of Pat's eyes. He took the cigar from his mouth, made a wry face, and ground it out in his half-baseball ash tray. Then he sat back again, sighing.

It was a Pat Garver that Cleve had never seen before. The pilot was usually charged with power, a dynamo of bursting energy. But now he was tired and defeated, an old man with the wind gone.

"All right, fellow," he said, sighing again. "If that's the way you want it, it's the way you want it. Go ahead and take your train." He paused and smiled ruefully. "Only do me a favor when you get back. Throw up a bunk for me; I'll be needing it soon."

Cleve frowned, not understanding. Then he forced a tight smile and said, "What's the matter, are you retiring too?"

"No, I'm not retiring," Pat said, shaking his head. "Not by choice, I mean. Maybe you haven't noticed, but this is the season for changing managers, and it looks like I'm next on the list."

"What are you talking about?" Cleve asked, his

frown darker. "The Wolves are riding along in second spot, and—"

"But we're not making enough money," Pat broke in. "Sure, we've been winning games. It's been a good year on the scoreboard and in the newspapers. But we've been playing to empty houses, and a team can't last long if the fans don't turn out to fill the stands."

Cleve dropped into the chair by Pat's desk and thought about it. "I don't understand," he said at last. "What's happened to the fans? The place used to be mobbed back in the old days."

Pat shrugged. "That's an easy one. We've got more fans than ever, but they just don't show up at the stadium. They sit at home watching the games on television. If we could just drag them out to the park maybe two or three times they would get into the habit again and see that it's much better than anything they could see on TV. The point is, we haven't been able to get them to come."

Cleve said quietly, "Are the other clubs having the same trouble?"

Pat nodded. "But some of them have pulled the fans back by giving away new cars as door prizes. That's what the owners of the Wolves want me to do, but I told them no. This is a ball team, and as long as I'm running it we're going to stay a ball club. I want the fans to come, sure; but I want them to come to see us play, and for no other reason. If that's not good enough, they can stay home and we'll go out of business.

"You were going to be my answer," he continued.

"The newspapers would give you a good play and the old fans would flock back to the park to see you again." He shrugged his shoulders. "But if you want to pull out, don't let me stop you."

Cleve was in a spot. He could return to his farm and save face for himself, but if he did he would be leaving Pat Garver in the lurch. The men behind the Wolves would be sure to get rid of Pat and hire a manager who would turn the park into a side show.

It was a hard decision to make, but Cleve knew that there could be but one answer. He said, "Get your publicity mill grinding, you old coot. I'll stay, but don't say I didn't warn you."

Pat smiled and said, "I've already phoned all the newspapers, and they ate it up. You'll be headline news in every sheet across the country, and tomorrow afternoon we'll have to turn customers away from the gate."

That evening after dinner in the Cort Hotel, where Pat had arranged a room for him, Cleve made himself comfortable in the lobby and glanced through the evening papers. They had all splashed the news, as Pat had expected, but the account in the *News-Journal* was the most caustic and, Cleve realized, the most truthful. It said:

CLEVE BREWSTER BACK IN WOLVES' LINEUP!

Pat Garver, pilot of the second-place Wolves, announced today that the old-time hurler, Cleve Brewster, has come out of his two-year retirement and will be on the mound in tomorrow's game against the Sox.

Brewster was once a great pitcher and a favorite with the fans. He led the Wolves to a full half-dozen victories in series playoffs and several other runner-up spots during his playing years with the club. That he was once a marvel with the sphere cannot be denied. But this writer seriously doubts the advisability of his coming out of retirement. It will be a sensation if he clicks, a black mark on his otherwise good record if he flops. And chances are more in favor of the latter, it would appear from here. Especially since Reub Crown, Brewster's old Nemesis, is now shaking his big stick with the Sox.

Cleve frowned at that last. No one had told him about Reub Crown being with the Sox, and he didn't like it. Coming back would have been hard enough without this, and with it the picture suddenly changed from gray to a dismal black.

The feud with Reub had started innocently enough. But through the years it had waxed hotter and hotter, to the point that whenever the Wolves met the Jays, Reub's old outfit, there were always more cash customers than seats.

The strange part of it was, Cleve and Reub had gone through the minors together with the Southport Eagles, and had been the best of friends. And they had put on such good shows with the Eagles—Reub with his uncanny hitting ability, and Cleve with his perfect fireball delivery—that they had come up to the majors at the same time.

Then things suddenly started happening. The first time the Wolves met the Jays, with Cleve on the mound, he somehow lost control of a fast pitched ball and bowled Reub over. He immediately rushed down to the plate and tried to apologize, but Reub came up swinging. A hard right smashed Cleve's nose and a pile-driving left caved in one of his ribs, and it was several weeks before the doctor would allow him to play again.

But that wasn't the last of the battle. At the end of the season, when the Wolves and Jays were riding neck and neck, Cleve received orders to get Reub out at any cost. He held the slugger hitless the first time up and made him pop out the second time. But when Reub stepped up to the plate for the third time Cleve knew he would have to pull all his tricks to keep the ball inside the park.

The count went to three and two, and suddenly Reub tagged one. He got only a small piece of the ball and it went short and high, right down the first base line. Glenn Nichols, on the sack, had pulled back and it was up to Cleve to take the pop-up.

He raced over, head up watching the ball, and put his hands out. But the ball no more than touched his glove when Reub crashed into him. It was a vicious impact, harder than necessary, and Cleve rolled end over end in the dust. It might have crippled a smaller man, but though Cleve was dazed he was not hurt.

When he got to his feet Reub was dancing off first, a grin on his face. "That will teach you to get out of my way, bum," he said.

Cleve dusted himself off and picked up the ball. But before he went back to the mound he said, "I'll see you later, wise guy. Right after the game, in back of the stands."

Reub laughed. "Don't worry, I'll be there. It'll be a pleasure to dump you again."

Cleve held the Jays hitless the remainder of the game, and then he met Reub behind the stands. They were two rugged young men in the best of condition, muscles hard, eyes clear, reflexes fast.

"So you want to fight, do you?" Reub said, laughing at him. "Never know when you've had enough."

"No, I don't want to fight," Cleve told him quietly. "But it would come sooner or later, and it might as well be now."

They squared off and circled. Suddenly Reub lashed out with a roundhouse right that almost tore Cleve's ear off and sent him sprawling. He jumped up quickly and shook his head, and Reub was on him again. But Cleve was better at in-fighting, and he sank his fists deep into Reub's stomach and drove him back, spilling him against the stadium.

Cleve waited for Reub to get up, and when he did it was with a lunge aimed for Cleve's middle. Cleve sidestepped just in time and smashed out with a powerful right that shook his entire body. And Reub went down in a heap, knocked out.

It had been a brief but brutal fight and Cleve was breathing hard and was still dizzy from the first punch he had taken. He staggered over to the red fire buckets, filled one, and splashed it in Reub's face. The slugger shook his head and sat up, his eyes mean, a scowl on his face.

"Any time you want more," Cleve told him, "just say the word. But no more funny stuff out on the diamond, get it?"

There were no more fights after that, but they still

battled it out with the tools of their trade, with Reub belting Cleve crazy one time and Cleve dusting off Reub the next time they met. It was a seesaw battle fought with grim intensity, neither ever really winning, neither ever really losing. And they had never spoken again.

Cleve folded his newspaper and exhaled. He didn't know how Reub felt about it now, with the two years that had elapsed since they last faced each other, but the fires of anger no longer burned in his chest. He had thought about the feud many times, up on the farm, and wondered why they hadn't tried to patch things up, admitting that it had all been a mistake. But neither of them had done anything, and now he was going to be pitching to Reub the next afternoon without knowing how his old friend and bitter enemy felt about it. . . .

The following day was sharp and clear, with very few scattered clouds and a slight cooling breeze coming in from the northeast. It was one of those perfect baseball days, the kind that come so seldom except late in the season.

Cleve arrived at the field early, and he was just pulling on his cleats when Pat Garver came in, a smile on his face as big as a wagon wheel.

"This is the day for you to crow, fellow!" Pat exclaimed, slapping Cleve on the back. "Just wait till you see how the fans turn out to welcome you back to the outfit."

Cleve looked squarely at the Wolves' pilot and said, "Why didn't you tell me Reub Crown was with the

Sox? Was it because you knew I wouldn't pitch if you did?"

Pat's bushy eyebrows lifted slightly. "It was in all the papers and I thought you knew. The Sox paid a lot of money for him."

Cleve shook his head. "I told you I made a clean break when I left the outfit. Last night was the first time I had read the sports pages in two years."

"Well, don't let it bother you," Pat said, grinning again. "It takes more than one hitter to win a ball game. Besides, I think you've got enough savvy in that arm to fan him. Look what you did to Parks, Kelly, and Hassinger."

"And look what Jim Lunt did to me," Cleve added. "The first ball over, and he almost put it out of the park."

Pat tapped Cleve gently on the chin with a fist. "Forget it, fellow, will you?" he said. "It was just one of those things; I told you that yesterday. Besides, Lunt is going to be the best puncher in the league in a couple of years. The kid is a whiz."

"Maybe he is," Cleve objected, "but—"

"But nothing," Pat growled. "I've never given you a bum steer yet, have I? Now get out there and jog around, loosen up. And then oil that arm when Newell shows up."

It was a good fifteen or twenty minutes before Joe Newell appeared, and by then Cleve was ready to stand still and pitch. He hadn't realized how badly he had fallen out of condition, and his legs were tired and he was breathing heavily after the jogging session.

He settled down and lobbed them in, again making them nothing-balls at first and slowly adding the twist. His arm felt better than it had the previous afternoon, and he found that the sphere was breaking with a more satisfying abruptness.

But he still didn't like the way things were stacked up. He thought it had been a bad decision on Pat Garver's part to bring him back for such a crucial game, with things tied up as closely as they were and so few games remaining on the calendar. But he knew it wouldn't be his fault if he was knocked off the mound. He would do his best in there, and if that wasn't good enough it wouldn't be because he hadn't tried.

The stands filled early, and long before game time they were jammed to the rafters. Cleve wanted to think that the fans had come back just to see him, to welcome him back to the field. But he knew that that wasn't the entire story. The fans had turned out mostly because they expected to see a knockdown, drag-out reopening of the feud with Reub Crown.

Pat was enthusiastic about the turnout and, in the dugout right before game time, he said, "What'd I tell you, fellow? Just look at that mob out there! I'd like to see any darn circus stunt turn 'em out like this!"

He went over the probable Sox batting line-up, and then it was time to go out there and get to work. But it was all too soon for Cleve. He had a peculiar sinking sensation in his stomach and his head felt light. He was a greenhorn all over again, getting ready to pitch his first game, and the willies had a grip on him.

One at a time the players slapped Cleve on the back

before they filed out to the field. They all wished him good luck, and Little Reed Little said, "Don't be afraid of letting them tag one once in a while, pally. We're not going to be out there behind you just for decoration."

Pat Garver finished buckling on his catching armor and walked out to the mound with Cleve. They shook hands, and the fans sent forth a tremendous ovation.

"There's your answer," Pat grinned. "Maybe now you know whom they turned out to see!"

And then Cleve was all alone, the lump back in his throat. At that moment he would have given everything he possessed to have his arm back again with all its old speed. But he knew it was too late for wishing. He would have to do the job with control and brains, relying on wisdom rather than brawn, taking his tricks where he could find them.

He took Pat's signal and pitched Biff Williams across the hands, forcing him back from the plate. The next one was still on the inside, just cutting the knees. Cleve varied the third pitch, putting it up to the shoulders, and the Sox leadoff man took an early slice. He got a piece of the ball but not enough to do any good. Earl Richards lumbered in from third and took it three yards outside the foul line.

Cleve felt a little better now. Williams had never been a heavy hitter, but he'd always laid wood on enough to keep him in the running as a constant threat. Knocking him down so quickly was a sign that there was at least a little something riding the ball. He toed the rubber with new confidence as Ted Conrad stepped into the rectangle and primed his mace with a handful of dirt.

He curved the southpaw high on the outside, and Web Diamond, the referee, called it a ball. The next one was better, an inshoot that caught the keystone-sacker unprepared. The count went to two and two and Cleve dropped in a ball moving so slowly that Williams's swing had passed the plate before the horse-hide reached it.

Cleve pitched away from Kennedy, the lanky short fielder, making him reach. Then, after getting him far over the plate, he fed an inshoot that knocked the batter off balance. He swung automatically as he went back, hitting into the dirt. Fred Veil scooped it up and made an easy put-out to Tom Jervey's big glove.

The fans whooped it up as Kennedy went down, giving out with a mighty thunder of applause and shouts, and the ovation brought the lump back to Cleve's throat and made his eyes smart. They were pulling for him after all. He tipped his hat to them as he left the mound.

Little Reed Little joined him on the way to the dug-out, a grin on his face. "Hey, you bum," he said, "I thought you were supposed to be washed up. You're better than ever, if you ask me!"

"Who in blazes asked you?" Cleve said in mock anger. "Save your breath and bring in a run for me."

But it wasn't that easy. They had to contend with young George Callahan's strong delivery, and he wasn't giving anything away. He tossed a brilliant mixture of floaters and curves, and the Wolves went down in order. Fred Veil grounded to Conrad on second, and Earl Richards couldn't come anywhere near it. Little Reed Little got a nice piece of the sphere on the third pitched ball, but it was just enough to land in Stab Dean's waiting glove out in right field.

"O.K., boys, let's pull a repeat," Pat Garver said as they left the bull pen. "Steaks are on me tonight if we hold the Sox hitless."

It sounded good but not good enough to make Cleve feel optimistic about the coming inning. Reub Crown was slated to be the first batter up, and Cleve wondered what might happen against his old rival.

Then Reub was coming out, wide shoulders, square face, and free-swinging arms jammed with power. He was a slugger's slugger, a ball player with plenty of weight to put behind the wood and strong back muscles and flexible wrists to push it farther. He walked to the row of bats with easy grace, selected one without unnecessary fanfare, and knocked the dirt out of his cleats.

Cleve watched every movement the big man made, remembering him as he had been two years, ten years, before. And he realized that Reub hadn't changed. The hair was a little grayer, perhaps, the skin a little darker, but that was all. The man was still the perfect machine he had always been, a baseball player in a thousand, one who knew every angle of the game.

He wondered how he could pitch to Reub, and immediately knew that he couldn't. With the old fast one he might have had a chance, but as it was Reub would belt anything else out of the park. He wouldn't be fooled as the others had been. His eyes were too sharp, his reflexes and timing too nearly perfect.

The tenseness spread even to the stands. The fans were suddenly stilled, the usual hubbub quieted. They were waiting expectantly, on edge, wondering who would be the victor this time.

Reub stepped into the rectangle and touched the plate with his bat, setting himself. He pulled his cap down farther and dug in with his cleats. Then, for the first time, he looked at Cleve, eyes squinted, lips unsmiling.

Cleve held the ball in his glove and wiped his pitching hand on his pants. He flexed his fingers and took the ball again, feeling the stitches. Pat Garver settled himself behind the plate, his face grim.

Cleve's first pitch was wide and low, and Reub let it go by. Then Cleve took the sphere again and shook his head. He had to keep his control; couldn't let Reub get him like this, or he would be out for sure.

He wound it and threw again, letter-high, right over the plate. And Reub took the bat off his shoulder and swung. He met the ball squarely and it started on a long flight toward left field. Cleve knew without looking that it was going to land in the bleachers for a homer.

Reub trotted around the bags and the fans gave him a big hand. The tension was over; they knew who was going to win this battle. As Reub left third he looked toward the mound again, and Cleve couldn't decipher the expression on his face. It looked like a smile of victory, but he wasn't sure.

Pat Garver came out to the hill, mask in his hand.

"What's the matter, fellow?" he said slowly. "You weren't pitching then. You gave Reub that run. On a platter."

"I—I know, Pat," Cleve said. "But it won't happen again. I guess I was just rattled."

"Then tighten up the bolts," the Wolves' pilot suggested. "We still have a rough road in front of us, and I don't want you falling apart."

Chuck Lions was next up, and Cleve worked it to two strikes before he blooped one to Little Reed Little. Then it was Steve Rogel, and he went down swinging. Stab Dean was the last batter up in the inning, and he put a hard drive right into Cleve's glove.

They went in again and Pat Garver said, "If Reub is going to affect you like that, better throw them wide and give him a free walk."

Cleve smiled grimly and nodded. "It'll be different next time, Pat. My word on it."

Tom Jervey was first up for the Wolves and Callahan wrapped him up in a neat package, sending him back to the dugout in seconds. He was followed by Don Parks, and he got wood on the third pitch for a long drive into center that was good for two on a slide. Art Kelly was next, and he let four go by before he saw one he liked. It, too, went out to center, and this time Reub Crown didn't miss. He backed up against the fence and took it in his fingers. Bill Hassinger was next, but he couldn't do anything and Parks died on the sack.

The score was still one–nothing when they went out for the top of the third.

The first two Sox up should have been easy, but though Cleve dusted Callahan without trouble, something seemed to happen to his control and he sent Gus Folbert for a free walk on six pitched balls.

It was a tight spot and Cleve knew he would have to knuckle down and take things easier. He had been trying to do all the work, but it was better to give them a hit and rely on the men behind him, than handing out bases for the asking.

Biff Williams came up for the second time and Cleve fed them to him, putting plenty of snap into his wrist. But Williams was not to be denied his slice, and he burned a fast one out to right field. It looked bad for a few seconds, and then Don Parks somehow got under it and rifled the ball to Tom Jervey. It was close and Gus Folbert came back in a slide, but the umpire jerked a thumb over his shoulder.

"Let's start moving!" Pat Garver yelled in the dugout, a scowl on his face. "Give me some action in there, and fast!"

Cleve was first to try but he couldn't touch Callahan. The youngster had a big arm and he pitched them in with unerring accuracy. And Pat Garver didn't have any better luck. He nicked a couple, but in the end the story was the same. Fred Veil changed it slightly and eeked out a close single, and then Earl Richards came up and fanned.

Cleve twisted them in to Ted Conrad, and the southpaw smashed out a wicked grounder, rolling fast and bouncing dangerously. Little Reed Little stopped it barehanded but couldn't hold on, it was that hot. By

the time he scooped it up again and got the peg off to
Tom Jervey, Conrad was resting comfortably on the
hassock.

Again things looked bad. Especially so now, because Reub Crown was still to be heard from this
inning. He came up just as soon as Bill Kennedy was
put away.

Cleve swallowed, watching Reub go through the motions. He was afraid to pitch to him, and he was afraid
not to pitch to him. Good balls in there might mean
disaster, and bad ones would be admitting defeat in
their standing battle. But Cleve realized he had no
choice. He couldn't gamble the game because of a personal matter, and Pat Garver had issued instructions to
walk him.

Cleve faced off and let go. The pitch was wide and
high, and Web Diamond stuck out a finger. Cleve
flexed his arm again, putting the next one in the same
place, and Reub frowned, cutting impatiently with
his bat. Cleve knew from past experience that the slugger did not like to walk and would do everything he
could to get his bat on the ball, and he varied the next
one, intending it to be low and inside.

Reub saw it coming and stepped back, swinging. He
connected, far out on the tip, but it was a good hit.
Don Parks speared it on the first bounce and pegged
to third, forcing Ted Conrad back to second.

It was one out and two on, and the Sox were still
ahead. It would take a miracle to keep the scoreboard
from changing again this inning.

Chuck Lions stepped into the rectangle and waited

for the pitch, his face set in determined lines. Cleve worked it to two-and-two, and then Lions choked the bat and bunted.

Cleve raced in and scooped up the ball and riffled to Earl Richards in the same motion. It beat Ted Conrad to the sack, but Richards's heave to Tom Jervey was late by three yards.

Steve Rogel was next, and Cleve still had his worries. Rogel was a tough boy with the bat and it was about time for him to lay into one.

He did. A deep one into left field, just short of the bleachers. Bill Hassinger was on it in a flash, throwing all the way to Pat Garver at the plate. But Reub Crown got there before the ball did, and Pat let it go to Richards. There was a cloud of dust as Ted Conrad came sliding toward the sack. He crashed into Richards and knocked him tumbling, and Cleve held his breath. But Richards bobbed up again with a grin on his face and the ball in his hands.

There was very little talking in the Wolves' dugout as they came up for their licks in the bottom of the fifth. They were grim-faced men with the specter of series money slipping from them unless they took this game, and when they went up to bat they went with a do-or-die determination.

And it paid off. Little Reed Little slapped out a close single and Tom Jervey was given a walk. Then Don Parks waded into the first pitched ball for a terrific triple that tied up the score. But that was all. Art Kelly and Bill Hassinger both went down on fly balls, and then Cleve took his cuts without connecting.

The Wolves were a jubilant bunch going out to the field, and Fred Veil said, "It's right in our hip pockets now, kiddo."

Cleve grinned in return, but he didn't share the keystone-sacker's optimism. There was still plenty of time for Reub Crown to come up again, and Cleve was afraid of what would happen when he did.

The game moved on. It became the bottom of the seventh with the score still tied up. As they went out to the field again Pat Garver said, "What about Reub, fellow? He's coming up again this time."

"I know," Cleve said. "I've been thinking about him, and I'm going to pitch to him. If I'm not good enough to put him out, he deserves to belt one."

"You've made up your mind? Definitely?"

"Definitely."

"Well, don't be so glum about it," Pat growled. "Give him all you've got!"

Hoyt Vine, who had gone in at second for Biff Williams, was first up. Cleve wasn't sure how to pitch to him, and he laid into it for an easy single and sat tight without trying to pull a stretch. And then Reub stepped out of the circle.

Cleve's face was tight and drawn as he watched the big Sox go through the preparatory motions. It was his fourth time up, and so far he had had easy riding, with nothing in there to test him. But Cleve was no longer afraid. Besides, he knew that if he pitched to Reub the way he had the last two times, the fans would raise a row that wouldn't do the future gate any good. And that would hurt Pat Garver. There was only one thing to do—and that was to pitch his best.

He sent the first one in high and wide, to keep from giving his hand away. Reub let it go and moved up closer to the plate. Cleve flexed his arm again, almost lazily, and then put it right down the center, spinning for a drop. It worked as he had hoped and caught Reub flat-footed. He unlumbered his bat and swung, but missed by a foot.

There was surprise on Reub's face as the ball went back to Cleve, and the fans were also mumbling their puzzlement. It was a switch no one had expected.

But Cleve was not finished dealing surprises. He had told himself and everybody else that the steam was gone from his arm, but he had not been sure. He decided to find out.

Reub got set, more expectantly, and the stands grew hushed. Cleve put his arms high over his head, glancing at Hoyt Vine leading off first, and toed the rubber. He held his breath as he brought his arm back and out with more speed than he had attempted in two years.

The ball rocketed down the alley straight for Reub's hunched frame. Then it broke with a snap that amazed even Cleve and thumped into Pat's waiting glove with a resounding boom, Reub's bat swinging pathetically after it.

Cleve suddenly felt like a youngster again, his gray hair and thirty-eight years washed away. He wanted to sing a crazy song and dance a jig. He wanted to yell at the top of his lungs that he still had a fast ball, and that now he could control it better than ever!

But he did none of these. He still had a ball game in front of him—one that he had to win. And he knew that the next pitch would be the deciding one. If he could keep Reub's big bat out of action this one time he would have no trouble with the other Sox, and the Wolves would take the game for sure.

Reub moved back and took another stance, digging in. He hitched up his pants and spat on his hands. He was as determined to hit it as Cleve was to make him miss. It was the old battle again, and this pitch would raise the hand of one of them as victor.

But which one? thought Cleve as he put his arms over his head. Had he just been lucky that last time, or—

The ball was flying from Cleve's fingers, and he turned his head, afraid that even watching would alter the ball on its course. And then there was a tremendous yell from the stands, the loudest one he had ever heard in all his years in baseball.

But what did it mean? It had come so quickly that he was afraid to look, afraid that it had drowned out the solid crack of wood against horsehide. He turned his head again; Reub was walking away from the plate!

Cleve pitched to Chuck Lions and Steve Rogel, but he never remembered throwing those six balls. The next thing he knew, he was back in the dugout and the squad was going crazy.

"What a faker!" Pat Garver exclaimed. "You almost tore my hand off with that fast ball!"

"I thought your flipper was for fish," Little Reed

Little put in. "Come here and let me kiss that gray hair on your head!"

"And the series is right in our lap!" Tom Jervey was enthusiastic. "What a pitch, what a pitch!"

They went out and knocked in two more runs before George Callahan was yanked and Al Higgins put in his place on the mound. And then Cleve went out for the top of the ninth and fed more fire down the stretch, burning up the Sox' bats as if they were matches. It was the ball game!

The lockers were a nightmare of commotion, and after they had changed Pat Garver said, "You can forget about that bunk I wanted, fellow. After a session like you gave them today, I don't think we'll be able to keep the fans away with pitchforks! And," he added slowly, "I guess while you're at it, you might as well be selling the whole farm. You won't have any time for it as long as you've got an arm hanging from your shoulder."

Joe Newell came over and broke it up. "There's a guy waiting for you outside," he said. "Wants to see you right away."

Cleve went out into the corridor, and was surprised to see Reub Crown waiting there, a big smile on his face.

" 'Lo, Cleve," Reub said a little awkwardly.

"Hi," Cleve replied quietly, studying his old friend's face and noticing the lines that had been put there by the years.

"Just wanted to congratulate you," Reub went on. "It was some comeback, all right."

"Thanks."

Reub shifted uncomfortably. "Well," he said, "I guess I'll be running along. See you around."

"Yeah," Cleve said. "See you."

Reub turned slowly and started to walk away. And suddenly Cleve knew they were both acting like fools again. He said, "Reub!" and the big man spun on his heel, his eyes bright.

"Put it there, you stubborn old cuss!" Cleve said, and held out his hand. And Reub took it and squeezed until Cleve thought his bones would be crushed.

"Hey, take it easy, you big gorilla!" he laughed. "You don't have to be *that* happy."

Reub's face was split in a wide grin. "You sure pitched me crazy out there," he said. "Just like the old days, eh, pal?"

"But with one little difference," Cleve said. "We can keep up the fight for the fans, but no more of that behind-the-stands stuff. We're too brittle for that now. Let's go have a couple of Cokes instead."

1504